PRIME EXAMPLE

THE FIRST RIM JUMPER ADVENTURE

I0619463

ISBN-13: 978-1-952412-18-9

Published By: Vagabond Publishing
Printed in the United States of America

PRIME EXAMPLE

CHAPTER ONE

He gripped the laser pistol tightly, raising it as he reached out to press the button that dropped the electrical field over the door of the small room he used as a cell. "Vacation's over," he said to the occupant. "There are some people waiting who have wanted to see you again for quite a while."

The unkempt man looked up from the bare shelf that served as a bed for "guests", his desperate eyes pleading with his captor. "Don't do it. You don't know what it's like here, what they do to us. Please."

"I'm not a social worker. Move."

The prisoner huddled on the bed, his body shaking all over as he muttered about all kinds of horrible things. The bounty hunter ignored the words. He got paid to find and return people, not care about whatever they were running away from. One of the things you learned early on in the job was that caring was bad for business.

"Move it!" He clicked the safety switch on the pistol, which whined as the power cells announced a full charge.

The prisoner finally leaned forward and got up from the bed, taking hesitant steps to leave the small cell. He wept as he entered the cargo bay of the ship that had transported him thirteen light years from where he'd finally managed to find a place that he thought was safe. A shove with the hand not holding the weapon kept him going. The exit ramp was only a few meters away; easy ingress and egress were an important factor when you dealt with transporting people who didn't want to go where you were taking them.

It was pitch black outside the ship, with the only illumination provided by a single light at the bottom of the ramp. The prisoner raised an arm against the blowing rain, losing his footing halfway down the ramp. He let out a short shriek that turned into a curse as his backside hit the textured metal and he slid all the way down. The two men waiting a few steps away shared a look of amusement before they stepped forward to yank the prisoner back to his feet.

Kole Anwynn stood just inside the ship, staring impassively at the scene as the muddied prisoner tried to fight off the men wrapping metal links around his wrists. At last, they had him restrained.

"Thanks for bringing him back," one of the men called up, his voice rough and deep. He had gray hair under the wide brim of the hat he wore to keep dry. "The remainder of your fee will be transferred as soon as we're back in the compound."

Kole nodded. He'd demanded half of his fee up front for this job, and it had been paid without complaint. He'd still keep his ship on the ground until the rest of the credits showed up, in case he had to provide a demonstration of why it's always good to pay your debts. He watched the threesome disappear into the wet night, then slapped the pad that raised the ramp.

Turning back into his small ship, the bounty hunter stored the laser pistol in the secure lockers with his other weaponry. He stopped to look into the small cell, sighing at the mess left behind after a full day's journey from the backwater planet he'd finally tracked his latest bounty to. Not that the sodden world he was on at the moment was much more cosmopolitan. Much of the galaxy's rim was sparsely inhabited, at best. It attracted the sort of people who were looking for freedom to do things their own way.

He spent twenty minutes hosing the room down, watching the filthy water circle the small drain that led into the wastewater tanks. From there it would be sent through several cycles of purification before it was returned to the potable water system. The system had been his first big purchase after picking up the ship from an auction, because water was one of the most important things you needed to have readily available when you could be stuck hopping between planets for weeks at a time. The efficient system could keep him going for up to six months before he had to pay for a tank refill from a spaceport.

Rim Jumper had started her life as a small freight hauler, the kind of ship some ambitious captain would buy and run for a few years on short trips until they could afford something bigger and more profitable. He'd passed by a ship auction on Nedelium IV during an early job, and he happened to see the rusted old hunk of metal sitting forlorn on a nearby pad. Something inside of him urged a purchase, and he picked the ship up for less than half its true worth. A previous owner must have been a smuggler who spent at least a year's profits on the interior retrofits that had strengthened the frame and created lots of convenient hiding places.

The rear of the ship was mostly taken up by the cargo bay. Nearly two full decks in height, there was enough space for fairly profitable loads. Kole had spent a lot of time reconfiguring it for his purposes, including adding on the small ramp that provided personal access to the ship. It was set into a massive door that could be opened to expose the entire cargo bay when large loads needed to be brought onboard. He had also set up a row of secure storage compartments, filled with weapons, armor, and other accoutrements that might be called for on a job.

To either side of the bay were tight rooms that held the ship's engines, powering the thrusters that could help his ship accelerate up to half the speed of light. The faster-than-light capability of his engines gave him a wider reach throughout the galactic rim. He could even make a full circuit of the galaxy if he wished, though it would take more than a standard year to complete the trip.

The inner workings for the weapons mounted on each wing were also located within the engine rooms. It was a tight fit when he had to wriggle around in there to do maintenance or repairs, but those weapons had saved him more than a few times through the years.

Situated along the forward edge of the cargo bay were doorways leading into two rooms. The medical suite was on the far left, a room that he had used more times than he could count. His shooting skills were second to none, but it was amazing how often a bounty contract led him into groups of people who all had a vested interest in keeping his quarry from being captured. The medical room was constantly in need of restock, and he spent a good chunk of his profits on those supplies.

On the far right was the tech hub, where the *Rim Jumper*'s network access point and computer core were situated. These were systems that he was frequently updating and configuring, ensuring that he had access to the latest data at any moment. Most ship networks could only reach for about ten kilometers when docked on a planet, but Kole had upgraded his systems to stretch three times that far. He also paid for upgrades that would allow his network to piggyback off any other nearby, extending the range from which he could keep in contact with *Rim Jumper*.

Beyond the cargo bay, the body of the ship narrowed in every direction. There was a single corridor, with a shallow ramp that led up and toward the front of the vessel. Not far along the corridor from the cargo bay were entrances to a small galley on the left, and an entertainment room on the right. Downtime was important, especially during the long stretches between spaceports when there was little else to do.

Next along the corridor were two cabins. Configured for a crew of up to four, Kole had never found a need to have anyone but himself on board. He had taken the one to the left for no other reason than he flipped a coin and it landed on heads. The second cabin with its dual bunks had been empty since he purchased the ship. He might toss a bounty in there if it were someone who didn't seem to mind being taken back to a place they most likely ran from, but that rarely happened. He mostly used the cabin for storage.

The final room on the ship, and the one with the best views in the universe, was the cockpit. He slid into the comfortable chair in the center of the small room that served as the ship's nerve center. Displays of varying sizes formed a half circle in front of him, just below the level of the wall-spanning viewscreen. At the moment, he could see nothing but raindrops slapping against the ship in the darkness, with the occasional flash of far-off lightning. With a wave of his hand, the screen filled with a thermal image of the surrounding area.

He shifted his attention to one of the small displays and pulled up the details for the account he used to accept payment on jobs. The credits never stayed there for long, being automatically distributed to half a hundred other accounts spread throughout the Rim. One never knew when one might need a stash of credits to go into hiding or get out of a jam. The second half of his payment hadn't come through yet.

Kole looked at the shifting colors on the viewscreen, trying to imagine how long it should take for the two men to transport their prisoner to the compound deeper in the valley. Unless the prisoner gave them more trouble than he seemed capable of, they should arrive soon. He decided to give them another half hour before considering his response to being stiffed.

"ShANN, what's available on the job boards?"

A holographic face coalesced over a small disk in a corner of the cockpit. It was a female face, with features that had been chosen as most pleasing to the greatest number of people. There were options to customize the display, but Kole had never bothered after buying the system for *Rim Jumper*. ShANN was the Shipboard Artificial Neural Network, an AI that he had come to rely on to manage the more annoying details of his business while he focused on the finding and capturing.

"Captain Anwynn, I have found three hundred and seven jobs available throughout the Rim. However, few of them are capable of meeting your needs." In other words, most were too far away or didn't pay enough to even cover his expenses.

"Anything interesting in those available jobs? This one was a little too easy. Boring."

"There is a job on Rigellius II, to recapture three fugitives who escaped from a work camp. Their suspected location is only forty light years away, on an uninhabited moon. Payment for this job is forty thousand credits, with projected costs being seven thousand five hundred credits."

"Why the hell would they go there?" Kole mused. He was tempted to take the job for the credits alone, but he'd worked with the religious order that ruled the Rigellius system before. They were zealots of the highest order, convinced that their version of God was the only correct one. You had to swear an oath to worship in their proscribed manner before they'd even consider hiring you. Even though it was only binding within the system, he wasn't a fan of spending half of each trip in a cavernous stone temple listening to chants and haranguing lectures. "Pass on that. What's next?"

"The second job is on the edge of the galaxy's Outer Core, captain."

She didn't need to say anything more. Kole had done a few jobs for the ultra-populated Core before, and he'd hated every second of them. He'd rather be in a Rigellian church. "Pass."

"That is all I can find at the moment, Captain Anwynn."

He shrugged off the disappointment. The one consistently good thing about being a bounty hunter was that there were always new jobs popping up on the boards. "Keep an eye on anything new and let me know immediately if you see something profitable."

The holographic face flickered and then was gone. Sometimes, he wondered why he'd even paid for that option. The most common interface was a simple image on a display, something you could work with in any part of the ship the system was installed on. He'd taken one look at the sales model's hologram and added it onto the bill. In his more introspective moments, he thought that maybe he liked having the feel of chatting with someone real. Someone he could turn off if they ever started to annoy him.

A ding drew Kole's attention around to a display on his other side, where he saw credits pouring into his account. Four thousand of them, making him smile widely enough to show all his teeth. The expense of finding the man wanted on this sodden world had been lower than expected, so he'd now have enough credits stashed away in his various accounts to keep *Rim Jumper* running for an additional month. He liked to keep at least a six-month cushion of operating expenses, for those times when jobs were more difficult than expected and took longer than projected.

"Time to blow this rock," he said to the empty room, as he swiveled in his chair to tap buttons that secured the ship and ignited the thrusters that pushed it off the ground. He flipped the viewscreen back to transparency, so he could watch the storm and rain until *Rim Jumper* passed through the thick cloud layer.

Stars seemed to burst into life, filling his view as he climbed higher. Even out on the Rim there were millions of them to fill the screen. Off to his right was the wide, bright ribbon of the galactic core, the place where most of humanity resided. Trillions occupied the worlds on the edge of the Core, while the population of the Rim could be counted in the hundreds of billions. The Gar Hegemony ruled it all, but their control of the Rim was more symbolic than anything. For the moment. There had been rumors in the last few years of a campaign to tighten the Hegemony grip on the galactic frontier.

As the small ship continued to accelerate away from the planet, Kole swiped through the star charts and tried to decide which destination he should set course for. The closest planet that was densely populated and most likely to offer plenty of work was three hundred light years toward the Core. Still well within the region considered the Rim, Kendril VII was a transport hub for people going even farther out. It was also home to stunning scenery that drew millions of tourists every year. Kole had spent a month there once with a female friend, hiking through dense forests and bathing under skyscraper tall waterfalls.

He was keying in the coordinates to send *Rim Jumper* there when the ship shuddered under him. "Captain, we are under attack." ShANN's voice was calm as she spoke the words through holographic lips.

CHAPTER TWO

Kole had already figured that out, and he quickly activated the projectile cannons on the wings. The weapons had auto-seeking programming, and he heard the sound of the machinery moving through the bulkheads as they searched for targets. He was trying to do the same thing, looking through the many external video feeds even as another spray of bullets slammed into the thickened hull of the ship. Warning messages popped up on his displays.

"Where is it coming from?" he asked ShANN, flipping through screen after screen of blackness sprinkled with stars. He stopped on a view of the planet he had left, wondering if they might have opened fire for some reason, but he was already out of range of any terrestrial weapons.

"An anomaly is detected in sector 2A-7."

He cursed under his breath, trying to remember what part of the space around the ship that would be. The AI system had chopped up a large radius into sectors, and there were hundreds of them. ShANN was smart enough to know he wouldn't have a clue where that particular sector was, and he felt *Rim Jumper* tilt as she redirected the ship in the indicated direction.

Kole looked up to run his eyes across the viewscreen, searching for what she might have detected. He finally found it half a minute later, a tiny ship that was twice the size of an escape pod. There was at least one gun mounted on it, and he saw the brief flashes as more rounds were fired.

With deft fingers, he threw *Rim Jumper* to starboard. The ship rolled away and the bullets passed harmlessly through the space he had occupied moments before. Kole pushed power into the rear thrusters, accelerating toward the small pod as his wing-mounted guns homed in on it and began to fire in short bursts.

The attacker's pod dipped, then shot away before it was hit by the incoming rounds. Kole was shocked at how quickly the thing could move. Half of the pod must have been fuel storage for the thruster. He adjusted his own course to follow, barely keeping the pod on the viewscreen as the stars swirled in the background. It was enough to induce motion sickness in most people.

"ShANN, can we get a tracker on this thing?"

"I will attempt to do so, Captain Anwynn."

Rim Jumper's inertial dampeners were working hard to negate the extra gravity being forced on the ship as Kole pushed his thrusters as hard as they would go. The pod was moving faster than he could, though, opening a larger lead every second as it raced away on a course that seemed to go nowhere. He tried to make out any markings on the pod that could tell him where it might have come from, but it was featureless dark gray metal. Perfect for blending into empty space and tracking someone who was accustomed to situations being the other way around.

"Tracker rounds are loaded," ShANN said.

Kole grunted, straining to push the ship a little faster as he ignored the new warnings messages popping up on his displays. He reached out to punch the button to fire the special rounds, and then watched the display for confirmation they had found their mark. "Come on," he said through gritted teeth. "Come on, come on."

"Tracker rounds are placed," ShANN said at the same moment the display next to the controls lit up with incoming data from them. With a grin, Kole throttled back on the engines and watched the pod disappear. As long as he was within twenty light years, he'd be able to find the tiny ship again. And he was going to do so.

Kole set course to follow the pod, chuckling over how fast things could change. One moment he was getting bored and trying to find a place to go where he could pick up a new job. The next instant, someone was trying to kill him. There wouldn't be any credits in it, but he damned sure wouldn't be bored until he found out who it was.

The tracking signal disappeared moments later. It was only a few million kilometers away at the time, which told him the pod had an FTL drive and had activated it. The signals from the trackers couldn't broadcast through the tunnels the faster-than-light drives created. Ships could only stay in them for short hops, though, so he could still track his quarry between FTL jumps.

Kole turned his attention to the warnings and found that his hull had been breached in a few places. The holes were small, but they would have caused catastrophic damage to his ship if they hadn't been automatically sealed by the internal protection systems that had cost him several months of income. He would need to pay for permanent repairs to the hull the next time he could dock at a spaceport with maintenance facilities.

The starboard engines were reporting a minor loss in efficiency, as well. Kole didn't like to see that, and he was on his feet and moving to the rear of the ship within seconds. He squeezed through the engine room, and after several minutes he managed to track down the issue. One of the bullets that had managed to pierce his hull had penetrated in the engine casing. A few centimeters to the left, and it might have destroyed the interior workings completely. The damage was in an awkward spot, as well, and it took him most of an hour to open up the casing and complete minor repairs to the damaged portions inside.

All the while, he couldn't help thinking that the person who had launched the surprise attack was either an excellent shot or incredibly lucky. The targeted areas would have meant lethal damage to any other ship, but *Rim Jumper* had been strengthened in all the right places. Kole had known from the start that his was a job that would lead to a lot of situations like this one. That didn't mean he liked the taste of it, thought, when it happened.

He was lucky the faster-than-light drive had heavier shielding, and that none of the shots had come close enough to do any damage to it. Being without sub-light engines was one thing, but potentially being stranded in the black with no means to travel to the nearest star without a journey that could take months or even years was another thing altogether. As he considered the shithole he had just left, he wasn't sure if creeping back there was any better of a prospect.

Two hours later, Kole was back in the cockpit when the tracking signal pinged on his system. The pod had reappeared two light years away, remained in normal space for half a minute, and then jumped into FTL again. Kole set course for that location, dropping a buoy that would receive any signals which might arrive while he was in the warp tunnel, and then activated his FTL drive. The stars on the viewscreen lengthened into streaks, filling his vision and making him feel as if he were sliding down a long tunnel with no end in sight.

Rim Jumper's FTL drive was faster than the pod's, but not by much. Kole stood up from his chair to stretch muscles that were sore after his contortions in the engine room. He had a few hours to kill, and the adrenaline from the attack was still flowing through his body. Working out all that energy was his first priority.

He headed down the ramp to the cargo bay. Aside from weapons storage, he also used the large space as a gym. He paid for expensive cellular regeneration treatments every few years to keep his body looking and feeling younger than his years, but still needed daily exercises to stay strong and limber. The last thing he wanted was to be chasing a bounty and get winded before he caught them. Or to be jumped by a few of their friends and not have the skill and flexibility to get out of the fight alive.

The first thing he always did before a workout was dial up the internal gravity field by fifty percent. It produced more of a burn on his muscles, building strength and endurance for even the toughest places he might have to go. There were a variety of weighted bags in a low chest, and he pulled out the forty-kilo backpack to sling over his shoulders. Then he started running sprints across the cargo bay, dropping at each end to do ten pushups from the ground to a standing position and back again. After twenty circuits, he could feel the energy draining away to be replaced by the euphoria he always felt deep into a workout.

He spent half an hour with a set of weighted balls, throwing them at a wall set up with a repulsor field that kicked them back at him to catch and throw again. By the end of the session, he had three of them in the air at all times, sprinting back and forth to catch and throw one before the next could get past him. It worked up a good sweat and let him work out the aggression he felt toward anyone who would attack him in such a way.

After the workout, he retreated into the galley for a quick meal to replenish his energy. By the time he slid into his chair in the cockpit again, they were getting close to the end of the FTL trip to the last reported location of the attack pod. Kole drained a bottle of water as he watched the streaks of light on the viewscreen. He was still trying to figure out who might want him dead this time. He'd made a lot of enemies in his years as a bounty hunter, but they were mostly the kind of people who tended to strike openly. They wanted everyone to know when they were responsible for a kill, to make others afraid of trying it in return.

Rim Jumper dropped out of FTL, and Kole turned his attention to the display that should tell him if another data stream had been received from the trackers. It took no more than a couple of minutes for his ship to communicate with the buoy he'd left behind, and the screen soon filled with information. A signal had been picked up from the pod only twenty minutes earlier, still on the same heading as the first jump. Once his reactor had stored enough energy again, he quickly dropped a new buoy, keyed in the new coordinates, and spun up the faster-than-light drive to continue the pursuit.

At the end of the sixth jump, Kole stared at the screen waiting on any data from his last buoy. Several minutes passed but no data started to stream in. He sent a small packet of information to test the communications channel, then sat back and considered the stars that filled the viewscreen.

The pod that attacked him had changed direction twice during the jumps, most recently on the final jump. It was possible the ship was still in an FTL tunnel, but it should have dropped out shortly before *Rim Jumper* based on previous jump lengths. A ship that small couldn't handle the kind of drives that would allow longer jumps and faster travel across the galaxy. Even his own ship wasn't large enough for them.

That left the idea that it could currently be traveling at sublight speed. But why wasn't data coming in from the tracker rounds implanted in the hull of the pod? The relay buoy would have picked the signals up as soon as it dropped from FTL, even if they weren't putting out any information at the moment.

"Perhaps our trackers were discovered and neutralized," ShANN said while he mused aloud.

"Sure, it's possible. I don't know anyone who would dare to exit their ship during transit through an FTL tunnel, though. How else could they disable the tracking rounds?"

"A sufficiently powerful electrical charge could short out the circuitry in the tracking devices."

Kole snorted, wondering what kind of madman would consider releasing that much energy throughout a ship filled with delicate instruments. Ships like his were shielded to survive electrical storms on planets or large amounts of solar radiation, but that was protection from forces coming from *outside*. Initiating a charge on your own would start from inside and fry a lot of systems. If the pod's pilot had done something like that, could they have survived it?

"The odds of survival would be nine point four three percent." ShANN loved to give him odds, even when he didn't always verbally ask for them.

"Does that include the risk of getting stuck in an FTL tunnel, never getting back into normal space?"

"It does, Captain Anwynn. As well as the risk of falling out of faster-than-light travel and having only sub-light engines with the nearest planet or outpost more than a light year away."

He was scrolling around the charts for the Rim, looking at the nearest possible destinations. There was a mining station a light year and a half farther out, set up to pull resources from a large cloud of asteroids that was theorized to have once been a planet larger than most suns. In the direction of the core were two planets, one three light years away while the other was only two. The farthest one was sparsely populated, still in the scientific exploration phase of colonization.

Kole tapped the closest planet, pulling up an informational screen. "Hebat Prime, single inhabited world of the Hebat system. A second planet in orbit around the sun, much smaller and completely barren, far out on the edge of the system. Let's start here, ShANN."

"Yes, Captain Anwynn. I will request clearance and docking privileges now."

He set course for the planet, preparing for a micro jump that would take him just inside the solar system. It would take hours to reach the inhabited planet so close to the large sun, but hopefully he could find answers there.

CHAPTER THREE

He had clearance before he was halfway through the system, assigned a docking pad at the spaceport on the outer edge of the only city on the planet.

Peak temperatures on Hebat Prime, called Prime by the locals, were nearly double what the human body could handle. The city was protected by a large energy barrier that blocked most of the solar light and radiation, lowering temperatures within while also creating a constant near twilight state. More than eight million people called the city their home.

It was the giant sun at the heart of the system that drew in the first colonists a couple of centuries earlier. Life on the Rim was hard, and energy was always in short supply. By setting up a series of solar spike farms on Prime, nearly a dozen families had managed to build massive companies that supplied power to more than three dozen surrounding systems. Their prices were half what the companies shipping energy cubes out from the Core would charge, creating a pocket of the Rim that grew faster than the rest.

The same families that owned the solar farm companies also controlled the planet. They owned all land outside the city, and rumors across the galactic network claimed they owned most of the city itself through shell corporations. Almost all of the eight million people on Prime made a living working for the founding families or their companies in one capacity or another.

As he approached the planet, Kole observed the slow rotation. According to the information he found, Prime had a seventy-three-hour day. That put the solar farms under a lot of light, but also meant the energy companies had to spread their farms out to maximize exposure and production. All but one percent of the planet's surface was landmass, which gave them plenty of area on which to set up the solar spikes that could extend wide sails to soak up the sun's rays. Each spike required a kilometer of free space around it, but then could absorb enough energy in a day to power a ship like the *Rim Jumper* for a few hours. Most of the families owned hundreds of thousands of spikes.

The city itself, also called Prime because the inhabitants were nothing if not original, came into view on the horizon half an hour before he arrived. He could see little of the city itself through the shimmering haze of the purplish energy field protecting it. The dome was surprisingly small for such a large population, but ShANN estimated the height at more than two kilometers for most of the protected area.

Several dozen landing pads were visible outside the energy barrier. Most were concentrated around the area Kole had been directed to, but a handful were scattered around the northern edge. Close to the large estates each founding family owned. He thought they must be private docking facilities. Even the poorest of the families could afford a couple of personal spacecrafts without batting an eye.

ShANN coordinated with the ground control systems to find their assigned berth, and Kole settled *Rim Jumper* onto the smooth tarmac without even the lightest jolt. He loved his ship more than almost anything in the galaxy, and he would go out of his way to make sure it wasn't abused. That was part of the reason he was still so pissed off that someone had fired on him.

A bubble of the energy barrier was extended to surround the ship as soon as it touched down, and the viewscreen darkened as the perpetual twilight set in. Kole unstrapped from his seat as a hologram appeared at the front of the cockpit.

"Welcome to Hebat Prime," the smiling man said in an automated greeting. His gaze seemed to be directed just over Kole's left shoulder. "We hope you have a pleasant stay, and we would like to provide several reminders to ensure your visit goes smoothly. Prime is one of the safest cities in the Hegemony, but we caution you to always keep an eye on your possessions. Often, people will forget where they placed an item and assume it was stolen. Most likely..."

Kole tuned out the words as he left the cockpit. He wasn't there for a vacation, and he knew very well how to protect himself from the occasional pickpocket or mugging. He stopped in his cabin to pull on a leather jacket. It wouldn't exactly be cool even under the energy dome, but he never left the ship without it.

A stop at the weapons lockers let him fill concealed pockets in the jacket with small knives for self-defense. He also strapped a holster around his waist, sliding a large bolt pistol into it. The weapon was older than he was, but well-maintained and regularly cleaned.

By the time he pressed the button to drop the small ramp, the air around his ship had cooled enough that he did no more than break into a light sweat as he left *Rim Jumper*. Feet on the ground, he turned to press a button on an exterior control pad attached to a landing strut. The ramp raised, and he entered a security code to lock down the ship and activate a couple of defensive weapons in case some idiot did try to break in.

He took a few circuits around the ship, checking on the damage left by the rounds that impacted during the ambush. The places where rounds had pierced the hull would need attention, but he was happy to see that his heavy hull plating had served its purpose and kept him alive. Credits well spent.

The next stop was a security scan. Two members of the planetary security forces were waiting just inside the door. One sat inside an armored booth watching a monitor that displayed the results of a full body scan, while the other stood just beyond the scanner waving him through. She held out a small container with the lid open. "No weapons are allowed in Prime," she told him brusquely.

Kole smiled at her as he unstrapped his gun, placing it and the holster into the box. He even pulled out a few of the more obvious knives that he suspected the scanner would have caught. Then he waited to see if the guard would ask for more. She didn't, closing the lid and presenting it for him to set his own code and thumbprint to keep the contents secure until he was ready to leave the planet.

"Enjoy your stay," she said once that was done. "As a reminder, your docking fee is eighty-six credits per twenty-hour standard galactic day." It was the normal time period, though the rate on this world was surprisingly low. Most places he docked would charge him twice as much and then tack on extras to refill water tanks or fuel reserves.

He was waved through into the main spaceport, entering a large echoing chamber that was very lightly populated. A group of about a hundred people were waiting in a seating area a hundred yards away, obviously ready to board a passenger transport to go home or get off Prime for a while. Most of them looked to be middle class, the kind of people who would save up their extra credits for a year or two and then splurge on a trip off-world.

Kole strode through the spaceport, heading straight for the door that was marked as an exit and ignoring the people trying to entice him to hear about luxury hotels or adventure tours. He wasn't there for a pleasure trip. He needed to find the local information brokers, the kind of people who could point him toward the person who used a ship barely larger than an escape pod to launch surprise attacks.

As he stepped through the sliding doors, the humid air slapped him in the face. It was hot even under the dome, and so wet that his face was covered in a sheen of moisture within seconds. He was regretting the leather jacket already but would never take it off and leave himself exposed.

"Hey, man. You lost, like?"

He looked toward the rapid-fire voice to find a young woman with pink dreadlocks sitting cross-legged on the hood of an equally pink hovercar not far away. There were uneven white stripes along the side of the vehicle, but he couldn't decide if they were decorative or remnants of poor driving skills. "Not lost," he said. "New."

"Well, of course." The girl sniffed and waved her hand at the spaceport. "Want a ride? I'll take you anywhere you need to go, man. I know Prime better than any, yeah?"

Kole examined her closely. She didn't seem to be older than seventeen, and definitely wasn't the sort to grow up in a family with the means for cellular regeneration therapy. Those people could look just as young well into their forties or even fifties. He wasn't sure how a teenager could know the city as well as she claimed. But as he looked around at the few other cars waiting by the curb, the exhausted or bored expressions of the drivers didn't inspire confidence.

Without a word, he walked to the rear of the pink car and pulled open the door of the passenger compartment. The teenager yelped in surprised glee as she slid off the hood and scrambled into the driver's compartment. "Where to, man?"

"I need to find a boss. The kind of person you go to when you want to hire an assassin to make someone dead."

She shrugged, the dreadlocks rising and falling with her shoulders. "No problem, like. I know just the one." She didn't even look at the screen displaying the traffic around the car as she pulled away from the curb, accelerating into the traffic flow. Several vehicles swerved around them, angrily blaring their horns. "Why you want someone dead, man?"

Kole couldn't decide if he was amused or perturbed by the matter-of-fact way she asked the question. "I want someone to *not* die."

"Oh," the girl said, a knowing tone in her voice. She looked at him in the small mirror above the viewscreen, her brown eyes sparkling with restrained laughter. "So, you go to big honcho, pay him to call off the hit, like?"

"Something like that," he said. Kole turned to look through the window beside him as they passed through the dim outskirts. Already the buildings were growing taller with every block. Towering high above, they would have blocked any sunlight even if the protective energy shield allowed more than a fraction of it through. Streetlights added a bit more illumination, but not much. The people walking along the sidewalks could see the length of a single block before it was swallowed up by the darkness.

"Where you come from, man? You not the kind of person I usually see on Prime, like."

He sighed as he turned to face forward again. He should have known she'd be the chatty type. "Somewhere else," he said shortly, hoping to end any conversation before it started.

Unsuccessfully. "My da came from somewhere else," she said with a wide grin that showed off uneven white teeth. "He came to Prime when he was my age to work on the solar farms, met my ma. They got married, and then had me, yeah? He still talks about the place he came from, but I've never even left Prime, man."

"You should," Kole said as he stared through the window, only half listening to her talk. Traffic was growing heavier around them, and he was amazed to see that little of it consisted of personal vehicles. The city seemed full of trucks transporting goods from one place to another, and taxis that must have been the main mode of transport for residents and tourists. They passed a few entrances to stairs going underground, telling him there had to be a subway system, as well.

"Where would you go, man? If you left Prime for the first time, like?"

He looked up again, to see her staring at him seriously in the mirror. "Capreed III," he said honestly. "You seem like the type to enjoy the more adventurous things."

She grinned again, nodding her head as the car swerved across three lanes to get over to the far side of the road. More angry honking ensued, though Kole had been hearing that almost constantly since leaving the spaceport. He was starting to think everyone on Prime was as reckless as his teenaged driver.

"Yeah, man. I love the rush of dangerous things. Me and my friends like to go up to the roofs of the tallest buildings and jump. What fun, man! The air rushes by, and your heart starts beating a thousand times a minute, yeah? And then, at the last second, you kick in the hover packs and glide down onto the street. Can't get enough of that, like."

She started to chatter on about her last jump, something that was apparently legal to do on the planet. From what she said, her parents hated it every time, always worrying that her hover pack was going to short out on one of the dives.

Kole kept his eyes on the buildings and people they passed. You could learn a lot about a planet by observing the people in their natural habitat. He saw a lot of slumped shoulders and expressionless faces, signs of a populace that was being worked too hard or not provided with enough stimulation. There were a lot of shops in the lower levels of the buildings, but he'd yet to see anything that would provide fun and amusement.

They turned onto narrower streets, and the buildings grew even closer together. He imagined it would be impossible to live in a place like this if someone had even the smallest amount of claustrophobia. Such a trait was probably rare to develop on Prime, where kids were accustomed to the tight confines they grew up in.

A few more turns, and they were in a part of the city that wasn't designed for hovercars. The road was down to a single lane not filled with pedestrians, and the kid had even slowed down as she navigated through the people and roadside stands offering food and cheap goods. Not long after, the car came to a stop and settled down to the ground as the engine was turned off.

The girl slung an arm over the back of her seat, turning to look at him through small slits in the protective barrier. "We got to go on foot from here, man. It's not far, like, yeah?"

Kole threw the door open and stood up from the passenger compartment. The air was drier here than it had been outside the spaceport, redolent with the smells of cooked proteins and starches. His stomach rumbled, reminding him that he'd taken few breaks for food while chasing the attack pod's FTL jumps.

The young woman shoved his shoulder playfully, earning a glare she didn't pay attention to. "You want some chow first, man? Best noodles in town around here."

"No, take me to the local boss. We can eat after."

Her expression brightened on the "we", and he realized he'd just implicitly offered to buy her a meal. It made her happy enough that he wondered how much she made from driving the taxi. He wasn't even sure how much this trip was going to cost him.

She turned to walk down the street, pushing past tight knots of pedestrians as she led him deeper into the city. Kole followed, bumping shoulders every few steps. The noise of all the people around him holding their own conversations was almost deafening, and more than once he had to go up on his toes to catch the pink dreadlocks moving ahead of him.

Ten minutes after leaving the taxi, the teenager stopped beside a door with chipped paint. She placed a hand on her hip, grinning at him as she waved the other hand at the door. "This the place, man. You sure you want to go in there? Pretty dangerous stuff, like."

Kole snorted. "How much do I owe you for the ride?"

She looked at him for a few seconds, her nose crinkling in thought. "Give me fifty credits, and I'll wait out here for you. Call the security forces if you don't come out again, yeah?"

He pulled a fifty-credit chip from a pocket of his jacket and flipped it to her. "I'll come out again. Don't worry about that."

The girl reached out to put a hand on his arm as he started to reach for the door. "What's your name, man? For when I tell stories about the crazy off-worlder who walked into Pulsar's lair without a weapon."

"Kole," he said, restraining a smile. He was tempted to pull one of his blades to show her he wasn't unarmed, but he didn't want to ruin the surprise for when it counted. Third rule of the job was to never take someone at face value. She could be working with whoever this Pulsar character was, helping to lure in victims for some scam.

"Neela, me," she said, putting a hand to her chest. "I'll be right here, man. Don't you worry."

"I feel better already," he said flatly, grabbing the door handle and pushing to open it.

CHAPTER FOUR

It was almost pitch black inside the doorway, and two hands immediately grabbed Kole's arms and pulled him deeper into the building as the door closed behind him. One of the people holding an arm pushed him against a wall, as the other one started to run their hands over his body to check for weapons. Those hands paused at a few of his knives, but then moved on.

After the thorough search, he was whirled around and pushed deeper down the hallway. He could see a faint light ahead now, the edges of a closed door outlined by the glow from within. One of his escorts reached past him to knock on the door, and it opened a moment later. Kole blinked in the sudden brightness and felt himself guided into an armless chair.

"We have a visitor," a low baritone voice said. "Who are you, visitor?"

"Kole Anwynn. I'm looking for the local boss."

"Anwynn? I know an Anwynn, don't I? Where do I know that name from?"

"Bounty hunter, boss. He's the one what got Leo and Jeremy last year on Pachel V."

"That's right. That was good work, bounty hunter. Those were two of my best couriers."

Kole's eyes had started to adjust to the light now, and he could see the people in the room around him. One man was sitting behind a desk directly in front of him, white-haired but thin and spry. Two others leaned on either corner of the desk, with their attention focused on Kole. "Someone attacked my ship two days ago. I tracked them to this sector, so I'm hoping you might know who it is I'm looking for. I'm betting they were hired to kill me, so who are the best assassins on Prime?"

The one behind the desk let out a short laugh. "I bet a lot of people want to kill you, bounty hunter. Maybe it was someone who was brave enough to do it themselves."

Kole shook his head. "Not like this. It was an attack pod, armed and equipped with the best FTL drive those things can possibly carry."

The two leaning on the desk shared a look. Kole could tell they'd immediately thought of a name, and relaxed as he realized he'd chosen the right system to continue his search.

The boss behind the desk didn't change expression, though. "Why should I tell you anything, even if I do know who might work in that way?"

"Because you're Pulsar, and I have a feeling this assassin is operating without your approval. Otherwise, you would have tried to kill me the moment I gave my name."

"Tried? I would have done it." His hand was a blur as it appeared from under the desk with a laser pistol, but before it was pointed at Kole a knife was already in the air. The blade passed only a centimeter away from Pulsar's head before embedding in the wall behind him.

32

The men leaning on the desk jumped to their feet, pulling weapons. But the man behind the desk only laughed as he set his own pistol down. "Okay, now I'm satisfied that you're really who you say you are." He waved for his guards to lower their weapons. "I do have an idea of who might have attacked you, but you have to understand that I can't just give you a name. People pay me to stay protected."

Kole nodded. "I can appreciate that." He thought about it for a while, coming up with another way to approach the matter. "Let's say I'm here to hire someone to kill my ex-wife. I want her dead, and I want it to look like an accident that occurred while she's traveling between worlds. I'm willing to pay for the best. Who would you suggest I speak to for that?"

Pulsar smiled slowly, leaning back in his chair and looking up at the ceiling. "I can think of a few people with the skills you need. None of them are cheap. For a small consideration, I can provide you with the contact details for the one I'd recommend."

The two men chuckled as they settled back onto the edges of the desk. They still held the guns in their hands, though, taking no chances now that Kole had proved he could be dangerous.

"Would two thousand be enough of a consideration?"

"Five thousand would be better."

Kole grunted at that number, suppressing his initial thoughts of killing the two goons and forcing the information from Pulsar. That would cause more trouble than he had time for, though. He pulled a small datapad from his thigh pocket, smirking as the other men in the room tensed at the movement. He keyed in his password to unlock the connection to *Rim Jumper*, and then accessed one of his bank accounts through the ship's server. It was an account set up on a system that insured anonymity. Accounts had only numbers, and no one was able to access the names of the holders. He initiated the transfer of five thousand credits, then set the datapad on the desk so the man sitting across from him could input the destination account information.

"Pleasure doing business with you," Pulsar said, pushing the datapad across the desk. "And they say bounty hunters are unreasonable blowhards."

"Funny, they say the same thing about crime bosses." Kole shared a tight smile with the man. "Contact details for the assassin?"

"You'll get them soon," Pulsar said. The two men leaning on the desk stood and motioned for Kole to leave. He pressed his lips together, wondering if he should insist on getting the information before leaving the office. He finally decided that he knew enough about the building to get back in if it became necessary to push harder later.

"I'll give you an hour," he said as he got up from the chair. The door of the office opened, and he stepped into the pitch-black hallway again. Hands grabbed his arms, guiding him along. He wondered if the two people holding onto him were wearing infrared goggles that allowed them to see. Or perhaps they traversed the hallway so often they didn't need to be able to see where they were going.

34

The chipped door opened after half a minute in the darkness, and he was gently shoved out onto the street. The door slammed shut behind him, and he blinked in the dim twilight that seemed far too bright.

"Kole, you still alive," a chipper voice said with happy surprise. "I'm impressed, man."

CHAPTER FIVE

Kole looked at Neela. The teenager was sitting on an over-turned crate nearby, ignoring the complaints from the vendor of the stall who was trying to sell the fruits that were in the crate. She looked genuinely happy to see him again, while he was surprised to see her. Once he'd given her the fifty credits, he thought for sure she'd take off the moment he was inside the building.

She stood to walk over, reaching up to take his chin in her hand at turn his face in either direction. Her fingers were cool against his skin. "Not a scratch on you, like. How you do that?"

He grabbed her wrist to remove her hand, fighting a twitch of his lips. "I made a very convincing argument." His stomach rumbled again, the smell of street food filling his nostrils the moment he was outside the building and reminding him of his hunger. "I guess I owe you lunch."

"Lunch? It's time for dinner, man." Neela held up a hand, tapping her wrist in a gesture that meant the other person should check the time. Kole had always wondered where such an ancient sign had originated, but he was never curious enough to research it even in the dull hours between FTL jumps.

"Dinner, then. You're the local, who does the best food around here?"

"You want street food, then we go over there." She pointed with her chin toward an elevated stand that had a line of at least twenty customers already waiting. "For better food, I know a place thirty blocks south that does the best dumplings in the galaxy, like."

"Let's eat here." He wasn't sure how Pulsar was intending to get the information on the assassin to him, and he didn't want to wander far. Less work if he had to bust in and beat the details out of the crime boss.

Neela led the way to the stand, recounting seemingly every bite she'd ever had of the food served there. The delicacy was something called rat balls, which didn't sound very appetizing. She insisted he had to try it, though, ordering two of them before he could say a word when they made it to the front of the line.

When two small bowls were shoved through the window, Neela passed him the larger one. It was filled with dozens of small brown balls that had some kind of coating that held the insides together when it was fried in vegetable oil. The girl was already popping them in her mouth, chewing with a smile of satisfaction.

Kole took one between his fingers, hesitantly putting it between his teeth and biting down. His mouth was filled with a meaty flavor, and a hint of sweetness behind it. Not bad at all. So he tried a second one. This time the flavor was more like a leafy green vegetable along with a spice that flooded his mouth with heat.

"Good, yeah?" Neela was already munching on the last of her rat balls.

"Decent," he conceded, popping a couple more into his mouth. "Are they all different?"

She shrugged. "Melo, he get whatever he can from the stores, man. Put it all together and fry it, like. Delish."

Kole wasn't going to complain as he kept eating. It tasted far better than he had expected from the name, and it was superior to most street food he'd eaten on hundreds of worlds across the Rim. Cheap, too, which made him cave to an impulse to give the teenager a few credits to get back in line for a second helping. She squealed with delight, like he'd just given her the best gift of the year.

She brought back a couple of bottles of blue liquid, this time. It looked like colored water, but as soon as it touched his tongue it started to fizz wildly. It burned going down his throat, as all the best alcohol should. "Fizz bombs!" she told him gleefully.

By the time the meal was over, Kole was starting to feel tense again. It was getting close to the end of the hour he'd given Pulsar to deliver the information, and he was already starting to think of ways to get through the dark hallway and into the inner sanctum. He was also eying all the loiterers along the street, wondering how many of them worked for the crime boss.

One of them, a greasy-looking man with stringy black hair and skin that looked like it was stretched too tight, pushed away from a wall after a while. Kole had seen him leaning there for most of the hour, watching the two of them eat rat balls and drink fizz bombs. Now he strolled over with a rolling gait to stop a few paces away.

"What do you want?" Kole asked, keeping his tone neutral while his eyes promised violence.

"Boss said to give this to you exactly fifty-nine minutes after you left the office," the man said. He held out a data chip, dropping it as Kole reached out to grab it. Turning on a heel, he disappeared into the crowds walking along the street.

"What's that, man?" Neela's gaze was inquisitive, locked onto the data chip as Kole picked it up from the ground.

"It's someone screwing around with me," he said. He couldn't help but smile over it, a petty power play that he could see himself pulling with the more annoying contract holders he dealt with. He'd seen the greasy man arrive only a few minutes after he left Pulsar's office, while he was standing in line with the girl for the first serving of food. He then waited there until the very end of the hour Kole had demanded to have the information by.

The tiny chip slid smoothly into the slot on the side of his datapad, and it took only a few seconds for the information to begin to display. There was a network address to send messages to, along with a procedure for asking the assassin to perform certain jobs. If you didn't receive a response within twenty hours, you could consider your job rejected. Whoever this person was, they were very careful about not letting anyone find out their identity.

"I thought you was trying to stop a hit? This makes it look like you going to start one, man."

"I have to find the killer first, kid. Then I find out who hired them."

She nodded, but her brows were furrowed with confusion. "Sure, sure. That's what I was thinking, too. Just wanted to make sure you had it, like. You going to contact them?"

"Just did," he said, after typing in a short message and sending it out. It was the same fabrication he'd given Pulsar about wanting to kill an ex-wife. He offered seventy thousand for the job, which should be more than enough incentive to capture the interest of a skilled assassin.

"Now what?"

"Now you take me back to my ship," he said, wiping crumbs from his clothing and then tossing the empty food trays into a recycling bin.

"That's boring, man. You come all the way to Prime just to see Pulsar and then sit in your boring old ship? Nah, I'm gonna show you what my world's really like."

He opened his mouth to argue, but the pink dreads were already disappearing into the crowd. Kole could only shake his head and follow behind as she led him back to the taxi, still parked where they'd left it. There was a fresh white stripe down the side, and he saw a group of kids down the block running a brush along the side of another vehicle. It must have been some way to mark their territory, or maybe just something they found fun to do, worth the risk of an angry driver chasing after them.

40

He got into the passenger compartment meaning to firmly tell the girl to take him back to the spaceport. She was already chattering away about the place she was going to take him, though, and he decided it would be more trouble than it was worth trying to talk over her. He settled back in the seat, letting her words wash over him as he watched the city pass by the window.

CHAPTER SIX

It was a short drive. The crowded sidewalks of the city's core were left behind, replaced by the crowded sidewalks of a less desirable part of town. The buildings were just as tall and glass-encased, with the same brightly flashing signs and advertisements covering them, but the people here looked less driven. Not that they were aimless, just happier.

Kole noticed it on a few faces at first, and then it became a flood. Instead of downward stares and expressionless faces, the people were looking ahead with neutral smiles. A few were even laughing as they talked with someone walking beside them. It almost felt like the day grew brighter around them, though he knew the same perpetual twilight covered every inch of the city under the energy barrier.

"What is this place?" he asked, watching a group of young teenagers laughing as they ran a twisted course between other pedestrians. A wave of smiles was left in their wake.

"This where people really *live*, man." Neela pointed up at a building as they passed. "My home right up there, like. Not high up in the snobs, but not low down in the reeks."

Kole craned his neck to look up, surprised to find he was genuinely curious about where the girl came from. She said her father worked with the solar farms, so he must be in a management position to rate a home in the middle of the building.

"Do your parents know you drive strange people around in a taxi?"

She laughed, a pleasant sound that pulled his own lips up in a smile. "They be worrying if they knew that, man. I tell them I work in a shop. Boring job, that, one they don't worry about or try to check up on."

He could agree with the boring part. He'd worked jobs like that when he was her age, saving up every credit he could until he was able to afford to jump into the bounty hunter career and get away from the rock he'd been born on. Then there'd been a few years of trusting the wrong people and paying for it, but he finally got the hang of the job.

"What are you going to do when you're out of school?" he asked. They were passing a sign for a local learning center, and he guessed it was the one she attended since it was so close to the building where she lived.

"Fah! School got nothing for me. I stopped going, man."

"You should reconsider. It's hard to find a good job out there without a degree these days."

The hovercar slowed to a stop at an intersection, and Neela twisted around to look at him with raised eyebrows. "You finish school, man?"

He returned her look, saying nothing.

"What I thought." She laughed and turned back around, smoothly accelerating away as the signal changed.

He could have told her to learn from his mistakes. That there had been many times he wished he had finished his own degree. He could have even pointed out that many low-level

43

jobs were starting to require it now as the Rim became more settled and the populations continued to grow.

But it would have all been a lie. There was never a time he'd regretted leaving school and his home in his late teens. He'd known what he wanted to do with his life and had never looked back. So, he kept his mouth shut and continued looking at the city as it passed by.

Five minutes later, the girl parked the taxi at the curb. Or within a meter of it, at least. She killed the engine and popped out of the driver compartment before he even realized they'd arrived at the location she was taking him to. By the time he climbed out of the passenger compartment, she was hopping from foot to foot with impatience.

"Let's go, man. Time to have some fun, like!"

Kole looked around at the people passing by in both directions. They looked no different than the people a few blocks over. A few even nodded companionably at him, and most looked at the girl with bemusement. Her vibrant pink hair really stood out in this crowd, along with the bright green overalls she wore.

With a sigh, he followed the teenager into the pedestrian throng. She went through a door into a building, down a long flight of stairs, and into a seemingly endless, poorly lit hallway. He kept expecting to hear the throbbing bass of music from a club or something, the kind of place younger people always seemed so fascinated with. A proper drink would be nice, at least.

"You go too slow," she complained, taking his hand and pulling him into a half jog. After a hundred meters, they suddenly turned into another hallway. And again, soon after. Whatever this place was, it was a veritable maze.

Half a dozen twists and turns later, they stopped in front of a solid metal door. Neela released his hand, which felt suddenly hot without her surprisingly cool touch. She banged on the door, three times in quick succession and then two more after a pause.

The door was pulled open to admit them into the last place Kole would have ever expected to find underneath a city like Prime. His breath turned to vapor a few steps inside, and the door shut quickly behind them. Neela was grinning up at him, enjoying the awed look on his face.

The large room had been turned into an icy wonderland. A small bar and half a dozen stools were carved from blocks of ice, along with a few tables and long benches. A section of the room was set up for people to skate on with bladed platforms that were strapped to their shoes. Some enterprising young man had also set up a long curving track with a gentle slope that people could navigate while riding on a round disk.

A heavy coat was placed over Kole's shoulders, and he turned to find a woman around his own age. "Welcome to the Ice Palace. Gets cold in here, yeah? Just make sure you leave it when you done." She then pulled another coat from a rack for Neela. The teenager wrapped it around herself, closing her eyes as she enjoyed the warmth of the synthetic fur that rubbed against her cheeks.

45

"Who is you?" the woman asked. She had the same rapid delivery and spoke with the slang that Neela used, and he wondered if it were indicative of those who grew up in a certain section of the city.

"Kole Anwynn," he said with a nod of greeting.

"Cady Burrows, and this my place. Since you with Neela, no entry fee today."

"I appreciate the generous concession."

"Cady, can I ride the sled? Please, please, please!" Neela was hopping up and down, her hands clasped in front of her face. Kole almost laughed to see her revert to childhood at the thought of a little fun.

"Tell Rolo one ride free. One!" Neela was already racing away with a scream of joy. "So, you big-shot bounty hunter?"

"Where do you get that idea from?"

Cady snorted. "You think we backwater people don't know you? Famous, like, is what you are."

"I'm not famous," he muttered, turning toward the bar. Seeing his interest, she wrapped an arm through the crook of his elbow and led him over. The young woman behind the bar hurried to meet them, obviously intent on impressing the boss by taking care of a customer who rated so much attention.

"In the right circles, you are. I'm at the center of one of those circles." Cady asked the bartender to bring a bottle from her private stock, and then leaned over to pull two glasses from under the bar. They were carved from ice.

Brown liquid was poured into each glass. Kole pulled on a pair of gloves he found in the pocket of the coat he was wearing, before picking up the icy tumbler. He touched glasses with Cady, and then tossed the drink back to let it all run down his throat. The burn was nice and smooth.

"So why you with Neela?" Cady asked, sipping her own drink slowly.

He shrugged. "She was outside the spaceport, and I needed a driver who knew how to get me to someone I could talk with."

The woman's eyes narrowed. "And who would that be?"

"She took me to a guy named Pulsar. Apparently, he's one of the bosses around here."

She burst out laughing, drawing stares from others in the frozen chamber. "Pulsar the boss of something, that's for sure. What he tell you?" She filled his glass again.

Kole took a smaller sip this time, enjoying the taste of the alcohol on his tongue. He couldn't decide if it was something he'd tasted before, or locally crafted. "I had a little problem with someone trying to kill me a few days ago. Pulsar gave me a way to get in contact with that person, so I can find out who hired them."

Cady was shaking her head, slapping the bar with amusement. "Let me guess? You pay him a 'consideration' and he gave you a name. Said it was the best of the best, like, and had to be your guy."

"Yeah."

"You out your credits, man. No way you ever hear back from whatever contact he gave you. Pulsar pull that scam all the time, usually when off-worlders come here looking to hire someone to do crime for them."

Kole wasn't sure how seriously to take the woman. His sense was that Cady and Pulsar were rivals of a sort. He hadn't gotten the impression of being conned while he was in Pulsar's office. It wouldn't be the first time someone tried to pull a fast one on him, but he'd come a long way since those younger days. Besides, he knew where to find the man again, if it did turn out to be a scam.

At the same time, it couldn't hurt to see what the woman might know. "Where would you suggest I look for the assassin, Cady? They were in an armed pod, and they slipped right through my sensor screen. I'd be dust in the black if my ship weren't stronger than she looks."

A scream of joy drew his attention, and he saw pink dreadlocks flying through the air as Neela zoomed around the curve on the round sled. Her arms were held up, fingers stretched out as wide as they could go.

"I know someone who uses a ship like that, man," Cady said slowly, also watching the teenager ride the course. "He's not someone you want to mess with, yeah?"

Kole smiled tightly. "All I want is to know who hired him."

"You tell people who hire you?" she asked with a raised eyebrow. "Why you think this assassin be more open about his contracts?"

"Because I can be very convincing." He finished his drink, flipping the glass over on the bar.

Cady was examining him with her mouth twisted, as Neela came running up to them. "You should go, man. Fun ride!"

"Maybe next time," he said. "We should go. I really do need to get back to my ship."

"Aww, you no fun, man. One more ride? Please?"

"One," he said. She was already racing off before the word left his mouth. He shook his head in amusement as she grabbed the round sled and jumped right onto the sloped course. Kole dropped a few credit chips on the bar to pay for his drink and the teenager's joy ride.

Cady placed a hand on his forearm before he could get up. "I'll ask around, like. Get in touch if I find something, yeah?"

"I'd appreciate it. My ship is the–"

"*Rim Jumper*. You think I don't know that?" She smirked at him. "Have a little secret, me. I knew you were here as soon as you were cleared for docking. Pay a man in the 'port to keep me informed."

"Why didn't Neela bring me here?" he asked. "You seem to be quite connected to things, for a simple owner of an amusement like this."

Cady winked. "What the girl don't know can't hurt her, yeah? Don't you go telling her."

By the time Kole was at the doorway shrugging out of the heavy coat that had kept him toasty warm, the teenager was rushing over carrying a drink of her own. He hoped it wasn't as strong as the two he'd had. She was giggling with each sip, and he realized what it was.

"Fizz bomb!" she shrieked, as he helped her out of the heavy coat. She carried the drink out of the room, taking large gulps as they made their way through the maze of hallways again. It seemed incredibly hot after their short stop in the frozen chamber, and Kole could understand the attraction of such a place.

Neela dropped the carved ice when she finished the drink, to let it melt where it lay. She was still as full of energy as before, now chattering on about the thrill of riding the sled. "Did you see me get air the second time, man? I was flying!"

CHAPTER SEVEN

Kole gave the girl another fifty-credit chip when they reached the spaceport. She gushed her thanks, almost blushing as she explained that the first fifty credits had paid for the entire day and more. "Use it to have all the fun I don't," he told her with a twitch of his lips.

It surprised him to feel a bit of sadness as he passed into the spaceport. He'd enjoyed his time with the bubbly young girl more than he ever would have expected to. Maybe he'd request her again if he ever returned to Hebat Prime and needed a ride somewhere.

The security desk wasn't far from the exit to his ship, so he stopped in to retrieve his bolt pistol. The guard droned out the rules, requiring him to check the weapon in again if he re-entered the spaceport at any time before departing the system. He barely listened as he keyed in his code and pressed his thumb on the lock.

Strapping the holster around his waist, Kole strolled toward the set of doors that led to his landing pad. He wasn't keeping as close a watch on his surroundings as he should have been. It was the only explanation for not seeing the two twitchy men lurking in shadows nearby. As soon as he approached the door, it opened upon recognizing his biometrics. The men then appeared in his peripheral vision, too late for him to avoid them.

"Keep walking, and stay quiet," the one in front of him said, as the one behind poked him in the back with something sharp. Kole turned to look at the one holding the knife, and he felt the point push against his spine. "Walk," the first one hissed, looking wildly around the spaceport.

He was curious about their motives, so he did as they wanted and led them through the doors. *Rim Jumper* was sitting only a hundred meters away, with a defensive cannon that had dropped down from within the nearest wing. There were divots on the tarmac, and he snorted in amusement at the realization that the idiots had tried to board his ship before he arrived.

Both of them huddled behind him now, knowing that the defensive systems wouldn't fire as long as they were close to Kole. He pulled out his datapad and keyed in the code that disabled the program. The gun retracted into the wing with a whine that sounded like disappointment, and the ramp began to drop.

The one holding the knife let out a whoop, rushing forward to jump up onto the ramp. He was halfway up when a stuttering sound issued from inside and he was thrown back. The man hit the tarmac on his back with a sharp crack, the front of his shirt covered in blood.

"Willie," the other one cried out, running over to kneel over him. "You killed him!"

"He killed himself," Kole said calmly. The bolt pistol was in his hand, pointed at the survivor. "Now, who sent you here? And why?"

The man's eyes darted around wildly, unable to focus on anything for more than a second. "Pulsar. He said to find out who you really are."

"That idiot knows who I am," Kole said. "Try again."

"I swear, it was Pulsar. One of his guys paid us twenty credits to get into your ship."

"One of his guys, huh?" He grabbed the man's arm, pulling him away from the body on the tarmac. "What did this guy look like?"

"Big. Mean. Like you."

Kole knew he wouldn't get anything more from this waster. His mind was probably destroyed by toxic substances, and it was a minor miracle he could put enough brain cells together to even find the spaceport.

He slammed the butt of the pistol into the back of the man's head, dropping him unconscious over the dead one. Then he walked up the ramp into *Rim Jumper*.

"ShANN, alert the local security forces that I was jumped in the spaceport. Offenders are outside, one dead and one still alive." There would be questions, but he didn't expect too much hassle. Every spaceport in the Rim had leeches like those two, men and women who thought newcomers were easy marks or that their ships were carrying all kinds of expensive things that could be carried off and sold.

Back in the cockpit, he checked his message account for a reply from the assassin. Nothing yet, but there were still seventeen hours left before the deadline. In the meantime, he had a new problem to deal with. Whoever hired the two tweakers

53

wanted something from his ship. Maybe they just saw a pay-day and were smart enough to get someone else to try it. Or maybe they were targeting him specifically. It could even be the assassin, checking *Rim Jumper*'s defenses.

"ShANN, anything from your search for the attack pod?"

"No, Captain Anwynn. There is no record of any such ship registered on Hebat Prime. I have looked through the arrivals and departures for the last sixty days, with nothing that matches the vessel that attacked you."

"You accessed records for all the docking facilities?"

"Everything that is public, Captain Anwynn."

Which meant she couldn't access records for the landing pads attached to the estates on the northern edge of the city. It was exactly the sort of place he'd store a ship if he wanted to stay under anyone's radar. But how would an assassin have contacts in the richest families of the system? Those weren't people who needed a few thousand credits a month in return for access to their pads.

Kole grinned, realizing he needed a source of local knowledge again. He stopped in the cargo bay to replace the knife he'd left buried in Pulsar's wall, also slipping a small laser pistol into a concealed pocket on his inner thigh.

When he lowered the ramp again, a crowd of security forces personnel were huddled around the two men on the tarmac. One of them whirled toward Kole, weapon drawn. He merely raised his hands and sauntered down the ramp. "These two tried to force their way onto my ship. I'm sure the security feeds will confirm that."

54

An older woman in the security forces uniform walked over to put a hand on the younger cop's arm, forcing the weapon down. "Captain, we need to take a statement from you. The feed shows the dead man was trying to get aboard your ship at the time he was shot, so you won't face charges, but I'd like to know what they were after."

"They put a knife in my back, and then were stupid enough to think that all my ship's defenses were external. That's my statement."

She didn't look very happy with that, but he didn't give her a chance to insist that he follow them to the closest security forces office. Kole reentered the spaceport, keying in the commands to secure his ship again as he passed through the doors. The external defenses wouldn't activate until the area was clear of the people working the scene.

He stopped at the desk to check in his bolt pistol, getting a raised eyebrow from the man he'd retrieved it from only a quarter of an hour earlier.

As he left the spaceport again and entered the city, he looked around for the pink taxi. It was parked farther away, and he could see Neela talking with a young couple that must have arrived on the latest passenger ship. As he got closer, he could hear her trying to talk them into her car.

"You want some place romantic, like? I know just where to go. Show you a sunset you'll never forget, yeah? Just have to wait another seventeen hours to see it, but you won't regret it."

"No, thank you," the man said, holding his girlfriend or wife close as they kept walking to get past her. The couple didn't even look back, their steps quick as they hurried toward another taxi with a driver who looked half asleep and bored.

"I don't think they like pink."

Neela whirled, her face infused with joy. "You back, man! Forget something, like?"

Kole grunted. "I had a little problem with tweakers." He told her about the men, and the person they said had hired them to try to get aboard his ship.

"Pulsar not that stupid," the girl said with a sniff. "If he want in your ship, he going to get in, yeah?"

"I thought so, too. Do you know anyone else who might rip off ships? Someone brave or stupid enough to claim to be working for Pulsar?"

"There's a few like that," she said with a grin. "Hop in, and we'll go check them, like."

The passenger compartment of the taxi felt almost as comfortable as *Rim Jumper*'s cockpit by now. He didn't even think twice as she pulled into traffic and angry horns blared. He felt quite happy to be back in that hovercar.

CHAPTER EIGHT

Neela talked about sports as she drove, going on and on about the football league championship from the year before. Seventeen systems were in the local league, and apparently the result of the final match had been very contentious. Kole gathered from her bitter tone that the girl might have had a few credits on the losing side, leading to a deep-seated resentment.

The crowds on the sidewalk were lighter as they drove through town this time, and he realized that it was early evening by the Galactic Standard clock. He'd been seeing the end of day rush earlier, though there was still a densely packed crowd entering and exiting buildings. Streams of people were going up and down the stairs that he suspected led to a subway system.

"Okay, man," Neela said as they slowed down to drive through a grimier neighborhood. "This one a tough hombre, like. So you be careful, yeah?"

"Always. What can you tell me about him?"

"People call him Big Sam, but I don't know what his name really be. He buys things from tweakers and pickpockets, like. Little stuff, usually."

"And you think he might have hired the two who tried to get into my ship?"

"He doesn't just deal in small stuff. When people like Pulsar want to unload something, they come to Big Sam, like. He has contacts in high places, yeah?"

"That sounds more promising." Kole examined the building, a storefront like any other in the city. Flashing signs outside advertised all manner of goods waiting within, including electronics to fit every need. The glass front was opaque, so that he couldn't even tell if there were people inside or not. "I'll be back," he said, sliding a fifty-credit chip through one of the slots that separated him from the driver's compartment.

The sidewalk was crowded here, and he had to push through the flow of people to approach the door. A fanciful script proclaimed it as SAM'S EMPORIUM, which sounded extremely old-fashioned. That was the trend out on the Rim, though, with colonists and even the citizens of more settled worlds embracing the idea of the galactic frontier being a place outside the hectic flow of the Core Worlds.

A little chime sounded as he pushed open the door and stepped into the shop. It was a lot smaller than he'd been expecting, with only a single counter half a dozen paces in. Various small electronic devices were displayed behind panes of plastic, with handwritten price tags attached.

"Welcome to Sam's," a bored voice said. The young man sat slumped over the counter, his head in one hand as he flipped through screens on a small display. "What can I help you find today?"

"I'm looking for Big Sam," Kole said, placing both hands on the counter.

"It's just a name, sir. Sam doesn't really exist." The employee had the monotone delivery down, and Kole almost believed him.

"He sent people to steal from my ship," Kole said, pulling a blade and slamming it point first into the counter. "So, you tell him he needs to get out here right now to discuss that before things get messy."

The boredom was gone from the man's eyes now, and he scrambled off the stool to run for a door that opened onto another room at the rear of the shop. Kole tossed the knife through the air, and it embedded in the door only inches from frightened eyes.

"You stay here, until Big Sam arrives."

The employee gulped, pulling his hand away from where it had almost reached the door handle. Seconds later the door opened, and a heavyset older man appeared. "Go on into the back, Dustin." The employee disappeared quickly.

At the same moment, the outside door chimed behind Kole. He glanced in the reflection on the plastic case and saw two people enter. The second locked the door to stop any customers entering, and then both drew weapons and flanked the exit. Kole smiled in anticipation.

"What can I do for you, sir?" the big man asked, a slimy smile on his lips.

"You can tell me why you tried to send a couple of twitchy punks to rob my ship."

"Why would I have anyone rob a ship?" Big Sam asked, holding his hands out to the half empty shelves behind the counter. "My business is used electronics. People sell me their old stuff. I fix it and sell it."

"That's why you have two people with guns at my back?"

"One can't be too careful," Big Sam said with a tight smile. "I'm not sure who told you I was responsible for whatever might have happened, but they were mistaken."

Kole whirled, a knife dropping from the sleeve of his jacket. He tossed it toward one of the armed guards, pulling his laser pistol with the other hand. The knife sunk into a shoulder as he pressed the button to shoot a laser burst into the knee of the other guard. Within seconds, both of them were disarmed and writhing in pain.

He turned back to the man behind the counter, gratified to see the smile had been wiped away. "Why did you send people to rob my ship? And why did you tell them Pulsar wanted it done?"

"It wasn't me. I swear." Big Sam had his hands up, showing that they were empty. "Who are you?"

"Kole Anwynn."

Fear filled the man's eyes. "Oh, shit. I never would have sent anyone after your ship. Anything inside isn't worth the risk of this very thing happening."

Kole thought about it, deciding he believed the man. He was a slimy fence for low-level thieves, not exactly a mastermind who would look to blame a rival for his crimes. The fact that no other armed thugs rushed out after he'd incapacitated the first two told him that there weren't any others. That alone spoke of a small operation.

He stepped over to the moaning guards, yanking his knife from the shoulder of the first and ignoring the yelp of pain. As he wiped the blood from the blade on the man's clothing, he picked up the gun the second guard had dropped. A cheap mass-produced projectile weapon, loud and messy. He dropped it with a snort of disgust.

"If it wasn't you, who do you think would be stupid enough?"

Big Sam spluttered for a few seconds. "It had to be Pulsar. No one in Prime would use his name in vain. He's nastier than you are, bounty hunter."

Kole kicked the injured knee of the second guard as he unlocked the door of the shop. Not looking back, he exited onto the street and slid back into the pink taxi.

"Was it him, man?"

"No, he's too small-time. Anyone trying to rip me off would have more than two armed guards."

"I don't know. That's more guns than I ever want to see, yeah?"

He laughed. "I guess so. What's the next name on your list? Let's see what they have to say."

They stopped at three more small shops, almost all of them copies of Big Sam's place to varying degrees. Each of them a front for a minor fence, who got wide-eyed when they learned who he was and started to spill answers to questions he didn't even ask. Kole was satisfied that none of them had the guts or the resources to pull off an attempted boarding of *Rim Jumper*.

They also all said that only Pulsar's people would ever claim to be working on his behalf. It turned out the crime boss had earned the name because of his sudden mood shifts. He could be all kindness and joy one moment, and with a pulse the anger and viciousness would be unleashed.

"You sure, man?" Neela asked when he told her to take him back to Pulsar's lair.

"I'm positive. No one messes with my ship."

The teenager turned to look at him through the transparent divider. "You dangerous, yeah, but Pulsar surrounded by lots like you. Not a good place to go even when you pay credits and he happy to see you, like."

"Don't worry, Neela. I know what I'm doing."

"Yeah, you know you doing something stupid," she muttered as she twisted back around and started the hovercar. "Gonna get yourself killed, man."

He smiled, amused by her solicitousness. "Don't worry. You won't have to explain to the security forces why you took me to my death."

"Don't care about that, me. You my best customer, like. Made more credits today than all month."

That pulled a laugh from him, as he checked all his blades to be sure they wouldn't get caught up in his jacket if he needed them. The laser pistol only had enough charge left for a single shot, but it should be enough. He could take a gun off the first person he killed if it came to that.

The street vendors were still out in force as the pink taxi pulled up to the curb. Neela and Kole exited onto the sidewalk, continuing on foot for the last part of the journey. He tried to tell her to stay with the car, but the girl only shook her pink dreadlocks and started walking.

As they got close to the door, he flipped her a credit chip. "Get an order of rat balls and wait for me here. If I'm not out in twenty minutes, you get back in your taxi and forget you ever saw me."

"I go in with you, man. They think twice about shooting with me there, yeah?"

"No. Trust me, they wouldn't hesitate. If shooting starts, I don't need to be worrying about you. Stay. Here."

Neela crossed her arms and pouted, but she nodded in agreement. He started for the door of the lair, turning back halfway to see her already in line for the food cart, eagerly bouncing on her toes as she looked around the people in front of her. Worst case, he'd die feeling good about making sure she wouldn't go with him.

The door opened before he reached it, yawning open to show the pitch-black corridor he remembered from earlier in the day. He hesitated for only a moment before stepping over the threshold.

CHAPTER NINE

Hands guided him along the dark corridor, and Kole wondered if they were the same hands he had felt earlier in the day. He'd come prepared this time. Blinking his left eye four times in rapid succession activated the infrared lens. The hallway became awash with shifting colors, two red and yellow human shapes walking beside him.

There were doors along the hallway that he hadn't been able to see before. They gave off a faint greenish glow, telling him there were people or electronics behind them generating more heat than the ambient temperature. By the end of the corridor, he had counted two doors on his left and three on the right.

A red fist reached out to knock on the inner door, the same staccato signal as earlier in the day. Kole blinked to turn off his lens before the door opened and flooded the hallway with bright light. He turned his head back and forth, as if trying to help his eyes adjust to the sudden illumination. What he was really doing was letting the lens in his other eye capture video of the room and start mapping out the dimensions.

One of the guards within pulled him inside far enough to close the door, and then raised hands to perform another pat down. Kole gave him a sharp glance, letting the light glint off the blade that appeared in his hand. "I'm armed, and I'm going to stay that way."

The heavyset man leaned slightly to look around him. "Aw, let him go," Pulsar said from his seat behind the desk. "Did you not read the part about how it could take twenty hours for a reply?"

"I'm not here about that," Kole said, standing where he could see everyone in the room with his peripheral vision. "When I got back to the spaceport, there were two sketchy little tweakers waiting to stick a knife in my back and force me to lead them into my ship. They said you hired them."

"Buddy, if I hire someone to get onto your ship, they'll get it done. Someone else must have used my name."

"Oh, and who would do something like that?"

"Anyone could have done it," Pulsar said, giving him a confused look. "I'd sure like to know who it was, though. Teach them a little respect. Did they say anything about the guy that hired them?"

"Yeah, they said he looked just like that," Kole said, pointing to one of the men sitting on the corners of the desk. A tall man, with a perpetual frown and heavy lines between his brows. It gave him a mean look in the right light.

The guy turned his hands up and shrugged. "I don't know what he's talking about, boss."

"Vin hasn't left here since before you showed up the first time, Anwynn. He didn't hire anyone to crack your ship open."

Kole smiled, an expression that didn't reach his hard eyes. "Let's say I believe you, and I walk out of here. I just want you to know that if anyone else tries something like that, you're the one who will pay for it. We clear?"

Pulsar frowned, standing up and putting his palms on the desk to lean forward. "Are you threatening me, bounty hunter?"

"I don't threaten."

Minutes passed, the two of them staring at each other with hard expressions. The men sitting on the desk looked back and forth, sharing uneasy glances with each other. Finally, Pulsar slammed his hand on the desk and dropped back into his chair.

"I like you, Anwynn. There's not many who have the balls to stand up to me like that. I'm going to put my people on this, find out who's been trying to get into your ship. You think it could be the person who tried to kill you?"

Kole relaxed a bit, letting his hands drop away from the closest hidden blades. "No. Someone competent enough to sneak up on me wouldn't hire twitchy street bums to try something like that."

"Unless he wanted to take your attention off something else," Pulsar said, raising a finger to tap his temple. "It's the kind of thing I would do if someone were getting too close. Distract them while I created some separation between us."

It was a good theory, one that Kole had considered at first but dismissed as unlikely. "Maybe," he said. "By the way, I met someone earlier who told me that you're known to pull a scam on off-worlders. Taking their credits and offering to give them information for some underworld contact."

Pulsar chuckled, nodding emphatically. "Yeah, I pull that one all the time. Those dumb schmucks who come out here from the Core, wanting some Rim outlaw to kill their spouse or business partners. There's no profit in jobs like that, and the last thing we need are Hegemony ships coming through here pressing their laws on us because someone buys a hit on the wrong person. So, I take some of their credits, and teach them not to come back."

"I just hope you know when to provide real information."

"Hey, you got the legit data, Anwynn. No one here is going to mess with *you* like that."

Kole grunted, then turned on his heel and pulled the door to the corridor open. He activated his infrared lens and strode confidently through the darkness. Footsteps hurried behind him, the escorts catching up halfway to the exit. Hands wrapped around his biceps, seeming to communicate their displeasure at his abrupt exit from the office.

He didn't wait for them to open the door, either, reaching out to pull on the handle before one of his escorts could get there. The escort on his left growled in frustration, and the other gave him a less than gentle shove onto the sidewalk. The door slammed shut behind him forcefully, increasing his grin of triumph.

Neela was seated on the curb not far away, trying to pretend she hadn't been watching the door when he left the building. She looked around as he stood beside her, eyebrows raised in mock surprise. "You done, man? Barely ten minutes since you go in, like."

"It wasn't a subject that required a long conversation."

"So, was it Pulsar?"

"He says no. I believe him." Kole sat down beside the young woman, leaning back on his palms as they watched the lines of people waiting to get a late meal. Or an early one, for those who worked overnight shifts.

"What now, man? I got no other ideas for people you can hassle." She grinned as she said it. He knew she'd enjoyed driving him around town again.

"Well, there is one more person I'd like to speak with. Someone I'd forgotten until I was in there." He jerked his head in the direction of Pulsar's lair. "Can you take me back to that Ice Palace place?"

"You bet!" Neela jumped up, shoving the last few rat balls in her mouth and dumping the plastic container in the recycle bin. She almost jogged all the way back to the taxi, and Kole had to snort in amusement. He wondered if she was more excited about the Fizz Bombs or riding the sled again.

During the trip, he considered his next moves. Cady was the only one who seemed to have known about his arrival before he even left *Rim Jumper*. Pulsar hadn't known who he was until he mentioned his name. He could have had someone hire the tweakers as soon as Kole left the office, but the gouges in the tarmac from the defensive weapons had seemed to have been there longer than that.

It would be worth asking the ice bar owner what interest she had in him, that she was notified of his arrival so quickly. She'd also hinted that she might know the identity of the person who attacked him. He wanted to follow up on that.

The streets and sidewalks were almost deserted as they parked in the same spot as earlier in the day. The lighting of the city never changed to indicate the day/night cycle, and Kole kept feeling like he was living the longest late evening hour of his life. He had to check the small display on his datapad to see that it was getting close to the end of the nineteenth hour.

Neela was twitching with unbridled excitement as she waited for him to exit the hovercar and follow her through the doors that led to the stairs. He activated the video lens to make sure he could find his way through the maze of hallways if he ever needed to come back a third time.

They walked through the tunnels for longer than he remembered the trip taking last time. It almost felt like she was taking different turns this time around, and he was about to ask about that when she stopped and spun around in confusion.

"What's wrong?"

"The marks are gone." Her lips were pouting out in frustration.

"Marks?" Kole hadn't noticed any marks along the walls or floor the last time they'd traveled to the club.

"On the ceiling, man." Neela pointed up at the bare concrete, little of which was exposed through the pipes and conduits running along it to provide water, electricity, and other utilities to the building over their heads. "You got to be in the know, like, to even notice them. They gone now, yeah?"

"Why would they have been erased?"

The teenager shrugged, her pink dreadlocks swinging as she shook her head. "Cady move locations now and then, to

69

keep security from finding it. But she always tell me before that happen."

Kole felt like kicking himself. The disappearance of the club only solidified his growing suspicion that the woman who owned it was involved somehow in the attempt on his life or his ship. "Do you think you can find the place without the marks, Neela?"

"Dunno," the girl said. Her shoulders were slumped in disappointment, and he almost reached out to put a reassuring hand on her shoulder.

"Try. Please."

She huffed loudly, stomping down the tunnel looking from side to side. He followed, trying to restrain a smile at the obvious sulk. When they'd arrived at the Ice Palace earlier, the door they walked through had been very wide and very solid. He examined every door they passed, looking for one that was similar.

Several looked like possibilities, and he tried to open them. All were locked, and none felt as cold as he remembered from when he exited the club. Even if the ice had been moved out, which he doubted, it would take many hours for the room to lose the chill of it.

A new day had begun by the time Neela came to a stop in a section of the hallways that looked like any other. She looked around, lips pursed and hands on her hips. "This feels familiar, like."

"How many times did you visit the Ice Palace?"

"Almost every day, man. Best place in Prime. Even got cheap rides on the sled because I ride so much."

Kole nodded, expecting as much. "Close your eyes." She looked at him skeptically, so he reached out to place a hand over her eyes. "Close them. Now, think back to all the times you went to the club. You may have been looking at marks on the ceiling, but I bet that after a while you didn't even have to look very often. Am I right?"

"I suppose. I always look because they pretty marks, man. But yeah, I saw them lots."

"Okay. Think about walking down the stairs. It's hot up there, but down here it's cooler. The air brushes against your skin like the wind is always blowing. See yourself walking along, making the turns and following the marks."

Neela didn't say anything, but he could see her eyes moving under the closed lids. Her tongue poked out between her lips, and concentration etched her face. She held out her hands, seeming to move them through the air like she was letting them guide her along the mental path.

After what seemed to be several minutes, she let out a surprised yelp. Her eyes opened wide, and her pink dreadlocks flew through the air as she jumped up and down. "I know where we are, like. The Palace is just around the corner." She took off running, disappearing around a bend several meters away.

Kole followed more cautiously, turning the corner to find her yanking on a door handle and slapping her palm against the steel. She was knocking in the same rhythm she'd used earlier in the day. "Come on, man, open up! It's Neela, yeah?"

He watched her for half a minute, until he felt certain no one was going to be opening the door for them. "Let me see," he said, pushing her to the side as he knelt to look at the lock on the door. It was a heavy-duty model, the kind that wasn't easily bypassed. That alone would have tipped him off if they'd passed by the door earlier in their search.

She watched with attentive eyes as he pulled out his datapad and attached a couple of wires to it. Then he connected the opposite ends to the nodes on the lock plate. He had a program loaded that would let him attempt to break the encryption, a program that had proven useful many times in the past.

The screen filled with lines of code, scrolling past faster than he could read if he cared to pay attention. Five minutes went by, and his knees were starting to hurt from carrying his weight on the hard concrete floor. Neela had gotten bored after less than thirty seconds, and she was kicking the wall on the other side of the hallway, emitting loud sighs every now and then.

Finally, the computer beeped, and the lock clicked. Kole grinned in triumph as he detached the wires and put them back into a pocket with his datapad. He pushed himself up, then reached out to push down on the door handle. It rotated smoothly, and the door swung inward.

The bar and stools carved from blocks of ice were still there, along with the tables and the skating rink. Everything else was gone - liquor bottles, skates, coats, and sled. Neela let out a long moan at the last, looking at the sloping course with longing in her eyes.

The room was warming up. It was still cold enough to send shivers through their bodies, but not as uncomfortable as it had been hours before. A steady dripping issued from the bar, where the chunks of ice were already starting to melt. Kole walked over to run his hand over the surface, and found it covered in a thin coating of water. Cady had cleared the place out not long after his visit, perhaps already afraid that he might come back.

"I can't believe they leave and don't tell me, like." Neela kicked one of the ice stools, steadily chipping away at the leg. "I thought I was a friend, yeah?"

"Does Cady have a normal rotation of spots she sets up in?"

The pink dreadlocks flew as she shook her head. "She just pick a place and move in, man. I don't know how she even finds them."

A lump he hadn't noticed on the last visit drew his attention, and he half skated across the slippery floor to get closer. It looked like a pile of old clothing from afar, but as he approached, he noticed pale skin peeking out. He bent to look closer, but only a small part of an arm was visible. When he reached out and touched the skin, it was cold and clammy. Not all from being left in the semi-frozen room. He'd guess the person had been dead for at least two hours, probably closer to three.

Kole rolled the body over, flipping aside the cloth that covered the face. He snorted as he recognized the second twitchy little guy who had jumped him in the spaceport. He must have reported back to his boss and been killed for his failure.

Now he really needed to find Cady.

CHAPTER TEN

Neela was sad about the Ice Palace being moved without any warning. Kole thought she was mostly upset that they hadn't left a sled behind for her to use on the still slick curving course. "When they move, how do people find out where the new location is?"

"I usually get told, like. After a ride, Rolo will tell me to head somewhere else in a few days. Like that."

"But surely there have been times you weren't around, and they moved without mentioning anything?"

She hummed over that, then her eyes got wide and excited. "Yeah, man! When I was a little and my big bro would bring me, the Palace wasn't there one time. He said we'd find it again, we just had to watch for the snowflakes."

"Okay. What did that mean?"

"I don't know," she said, her face falling. "He just suddenly found it a few days later. I remember the marks that time were snowflakes." Neela was looking up at the ceiling wistfully. "Kole, are snowflakes a real thing? Do they actually fall from the sky on other planets, like?"

"They do," he said absently, trying to figure out how this information could help. "Neela, were the markers snowflakes this time, as well?"

Her pink dreadlocks shook. "No, man, it was a unicorn." Her eyes got wide. "Kole, do unicorns really exist, too?"

"Not that I've seen. Unless you want to consider scaly lizards with horns as long as their bodies unicorns."

"Man, that's gross." She shivered at the thought of them, and he almost laughed.

"Neela, did they ever mention what the markers would be the next time the Ice Palace moved? Or do they have a rotating list of them?"

The teenager was kicking the leg of another stool now, having cracked two legs of the last one to send it crashing to the ground. "Um, I remember after the snowflakes it was a solar spike. That's a weird one, like. Why something that gets ultra-hot, yeah?"

"Uh huh," Kole rolled his hand in the air, urging her on.

"After that was the unicorn. Then it was the dragon breathing fire." Her mouth dropped open, and she turned to look at him.

"No, I've never seen anything that looked like a fairy tale dragon before. What was after that?"

"Then it was the comet, like. Sparkly tail and everything. I loved following those. After that was the..." She stopped and bounced up and down with her fists held tight to her chest. "Kole, after that was the snowflake!"

"Very good. It would appear there is a pattern to the symbols. By that logic we should look for the dragon to find the new location of the Ice Palace." He looked around the room, giving it a last glance to make sure he hadn't missed anything that could be a clue in locating Cady. Finding nothing, he gently pulled Neela along and left the room. They left the door wide open, letting the cold air seep out into the hallway.

"Where do we start?" the teenager asked as they climbed the stairs to leave the underground warren.

"That's my question to you. How does Cady advertise the new locations? Is the marker symbol outside as well as inside the area?"

"Yeah, man. But you have to know where to look first. It's not a big flashing sign, like."

He laughed, unable to contain it. "No, I guess it wouldn't be." Kole noticed how sparse the pedestrian traffic was, and he was reminded of how late it was. Or how early. "Aren't your parents going to worry that you're not home yet?"

Neela looked up at him with a feigned look of indifference. "Nah, man, they not uptight like that. I go home when I go home, like. Where you want me to take you now?"

He could tell she was hiding the truth, but he didn't have the inclination to dig into it. Personal problems should stay that way, in his opinion. "Take me back to the spaceport." Her face started to fall with disappointment. "But after you get some rest, I want you to comb the city. Find that dragon marker and contact me as soon as you do. I need to talk to Cady about something very important."

She was much happier with that request, almost running to beat him back to the pink taxi. As he slid into the passenger compartment, Kole wondered if the pink hair was to match the hovercar or vice versa. Every other taxi he'd seen while traveling the city was white or red with yellow lettering.

77

Traffic was almost non-existent at that hour, and they made good time back to the spaceport. The long line of hovercar taxis was still in place, but there were only a handful of new arrivals approaching to get rides to other areas of Prime. Neela pulled up to the curb near the door closest to *Rim Jumper*'s dock.

"I'll start looking right now, man. Call you quick quick if I find a dragon."

"You'll go home and get some sleep," he said firmly. "Then wake up fresh and start the search. I don't need you missing the marker because your eyes are unfocused due to exhaustion." He slid a hundred-credit chip through a slot in the divider. "Consider yourself booked for at least the next day. Think your boss will be okay with that?"

"Sure, man. No problems."

His lips curled upward as Kole slid out of the passenger compartment. He raised a hand as the pink taxi pulled away and accelerated quickly into the flow of vehicles, few enough of them this time to prevent the angry honking. He hoped he wasn't making a mistake by putting the girl on the search.

After a couple of hours in his bunk, Kole was in the cockpit with a full mug of kaff before the seventh hour of the day. As soon as he boarded the ship, he had given ShANN the search criteria. She started combing Hebat Prime's entertainment feeds and advertising systems for any trace of a dragon marker. It was a popular symbol across the Rim, but he felt confident Cady would advertise in some way for those in the know to find the new Ice Palace location.

He'd also asked ShANN to search the records for everyone with the first name of Cady, including the dozens of names that could be shortened to such. The results would be in the thousands, but it was surprising how often he was able to find someone with a simple scan of their names.

"What have you got for me?" he asked as he settled into his chair.

"Captain Anwynn, I have found more than seven thousand instances of dragon imagery used across entertainment programs and advertisements within the last three months."

"We don't need to go that far back. Let's try narrowing it down to just the last three days."

He sipped his kaff, enjoying the aromatic steam that billowed from the mug as he held it close to his face. "Narrowing the search parameters yields five hundred and nineteen results," ShANN announced after half a minute.

Still far more than he had hoped for. "Okay, let's see if we can chop more off that. Remove anything that has been ongoing. Any ads for companies that have been using the symbol going back before the three-day window."

The holographic face shimmered as the AI processed his request. While he waited, Kole pulled up his messaging system. There was a message from Neela, sent only two hours after she dropped him off at the spaceport. He shook his head at the almost incoherent message filled with half-spelled words and jittering icons. If he had the local speak down, she had started the search after no more than an hour-long nap.

He was starting to wonder about her parents. He'd never been one to have paternal instincts, but he felt that most parents would be more attentive to their children.

"Captain Anwynn, the new parameters have reduced our results to twenty-seven instances."

He sat forward, looking at ShANN with a smile. "That's much better. Let's start going through them."

The displays around him filled with the results of the search, and he swiped through them one by one. There were several concert announcements for a new band that used a red dragon with widespread wings for their logo. He decided pretty quickly that they were irrelevant to what he was looking for.

A few others were from menus of rice and noodle shops, the kind of small places that were forever appearing and disappearing to be replaced by something else. Those were more probable to be a front for something like the Ice Palace, but they also required a lot of lead time to get operational.

The most promising were pictures of graffiti posted across some planetary social sites. The pictures all seemed to be of three different locations, and the artwork was elaborate enough to draw praise from passersby and questions of who the artist was. Kole brought up a map of Prime, plugging in the approximate locations of the pictures. Three red dots appeared, and the map zoomed in to show that all were very close to each other. Perhaps a few blocks separated them.

"That has to be it," he said, manipulating the map to see what else was around the area. It was outside the city's core, but not by much. Crowded with businesses and residences, it was the kind of area where an influx of new people wouldn't be noticed.

He turned back to his messaging program and pulled up Neela's details. "ShANN, I need an audio or visual connection with this person. See what you can do." While he waited, he typed up a quick message, asking her to meet him at the spaceport as soon as possible. He hadn't seen any sign that she carried a datapad the day before, though he had noted the small screen on the hovercar's dash that never seemed to be turned on.

"Captain Anwynn, I have attempted to reach the contact without success. My connection request was not answered."

"Keep trying. Let me know if you get a response."

Kole jumped out of his seat and headed back to his cabin. He pulled up his messages on the display over his small desk, and then went to the shower to clean up. By the time he was out and had shaved a day of scruff from his face, there still was no response from the young woman. He really hoped she hadn't tried to do too much on her own and gotten into trouble. He pulled on fresh clothes, sliding his arms into the sleeves of his leather jacket as he returned to the cockpit.

"Anything, ShANN?"

"No response, Captain Anwynn."

He sighed. "Keep it going until she picks up. Route it to my datapad when she does."

The shimmering face turned and nodded in his direction. He jogged down the hallway to the cargo bay, opened the doors of his weapons locker, and considered what he might need. The hidden pockets of his jacket were already stuffed with knives, and the security forces would scan him again for anything more lethal. Finally, he selected a stun baton that could slide into a thin pocket on his thigh. It would extend to become a meter-long stick, and with the touch of a button he could send fifty thousand volts through the end.

There was no one waiting when he walked down the ramp to exit *Rim Jumper*. The blood had been washed away from the day before, and the chipped concrete from the rounds fired by his defensive guns had been patched overnight. If nothing else, Hebat Prime went out of their way to keep visiting captains and crews happy with their docking situation.

When he walked through the doors into the spaceport, the scanners ran over his body. The knives and stun baton were protected behind strips of material that blocked the signals from all but the most sophisticated security systems. The kind that were far too expensive for a planet on the Rim. He waved at the two security forces guards sitting at their desk as he passed them.

Kole hoped to see the pink taxi when he exited the spaceport, but it was nowhere in sight. He hesitated, tempted to wait for Neela to respond to his message or ShANN's communication request. But he was starting to get impatient. If the person who had tried to kill him was on the planet, he wanted to catch up to them before they caught him.

82

He approached the nearest hover taxi, where the driver was leaning against the side of the vehicle with his head down and eyes closed. He jumped when Kole slapped the roof of the car, rushing to open the passenger door. "Where you need to go, man?"

CHAPTER ELEVEN

Kole was dropped off a block from one of the graffiti locations. He paid the driver the eight credits requested, having to admire Neela for recognizing that he would overpay and never mentioning a price for her own services. Of course, she could have crossed Prime in half the time the staid old taxi driver just had.

He looked along the street, searching for anything that might stand out as the entrance to whatever location had been selected to host the Ice Palace. Seeing nothing, he walked along the sidewalk until he found the first graffiti dragon. It was more like a snake with small wings, mouth open and flames shooting out. The body of the reptile formed a backward S.

The map on his datapad directed him to the second graffiti location, and he watched along the way for any other signs of the marker. Perhaps a small logo on a building, drawn in dust on a filthy window of a vacant space, or chalked on the sidewalk.

Nothing.

The second dragon looked exactly like the first, except for the color. Green for the first, blue for the second. He wondered if that might be some kind of clue for those in the know about the Ice Palace, something to tell them if they should turn one way or if they were getting closer or farther from the location.

On the way to the third piece of graffiti, ShANN buzzed his datapad. When he pulled it from the pocket he kept it in, a familiar face with pink dreadlocks filled the screen.

"Where are you, man? I'm at the spaceport, like."

"Where have you been, Neela? Why weren't you answering the communication requests?"

"Got busy, yeah? Walked the reeker's district, had some fish, looked for dragons. Didn't see any."

He didn't even want to ask where a planet without any oceans got fish from. Or worse, what local animals they decided to call fish. "I found some markings, and I need you to look at them to tell me if they look like the markers you've seen before. How fast can you get here?"

"See you in twenty, man," she said when he told her where he was. Then she cut the connection abruptly, and Kole was left to shake his head in wonder. He almost searched the local network to find out what part of town would be called the "reeker's district", but based on the local dialect he could only guess it wasn't the kind of place a young woman should be going into alone.

While he waited, Kole walked the block and a half to the final dragon graffiti. This one was orange, with blue flames. It was an interesting color scheme. As he stood looking at it, several people passing by glanced up and then came to a stop to hold up their datapads and capture the image. Those pictures would undoubtedly be spread across the planetary social networks soon.

The pink taxi arrived in less than the expected twenty minutes, settling to the ground with a slight screech when the engines were turned off. Neela climbed out of the driver's compartment and hurried over with a wide grin on her face. "Kole, you found it!"

"This matches the marker symbols you followed the last time the dragon was used?"

"Totally, man. Except for the color." She tilted her head to look at the graffiti. "Should be blue, yeah. With orange flames."

"There was one like that," he said, leading her back along his path to where the second dragon was located. She talked the entire time, telling him about her searches that morning.

"…and then this kid, like, just comes up and starts hassling me. Said I was on his turf, man, and had to leave. When I told him that all of Prime is my turf, he wanted to fight."

"Hmm, and did you fight him over this turf?"

"Naw, man. No point. I give him a few credits, he walk with me and keep the other pests away." She grinned triumphantly up at him. Kole had to work hard to keep his expression neutral. Something about the girl's enthusiastic approach to every little thing made him want to share her joy.

"No dragons to be found, though?"

"Not one that looked right. But you found them, man. How you do that?"

"My ship's AI searched the planet's networks for any imagery related to dragons. We narrowed down the options, and these stood out." They'd arrived at the second piece of graffiti, and Neela skipped forward to run her hands over the blue dragon. She nodded, then looked around the area.

With a happy cry, she sprinted over to a row of plants in large pots that had to weigh as much as she did. The leaves of each plant were intertwined, screening anything behind them. The teenager pushed through and disappeared into the foliage, and then a few seconds later her excited face reappeared, and she waved for him to follow.

Kole approached the area cautiously, trying to get a glimpse through the broad fronds at what was behind them. He was about to push through when a small hand grabbed his wrist and yanked him forward.

"Come on, man. Got to ride the sled again, yeah?"

He helped Neela pull open a heavy steel door, set at a slant to protect stairs that led underground again. Kole wondered if the Ice Palace locations were always under the city. It was probably an effective way to keep the room cooler and reduce costs to maintain a low temperature.

The steel doors opened without a squeak, letting him know they'd been oiled in anticipation of frequent use. The stairs were clean of the usual detritus and dirt that seemed to always accumulate in such areas, as well. Even better, there was another orange dragon drawn on the inside of one of the doors.

Neela was clattering down the stairs before Kole even had time to peer into the darkness for any kind of traps or surveillance devices. He almost called out a warning, but he knew she wouldn't stop. The kid was focused on one thing, and she couldn't even conceive of the danger that Cady seemed to embody. He followed, keeping the outer doors open in case they needed a quick exit. It didn't matter to him if someone found the entry and wandered in uninvited.

"Come on, man!" Neela was clearly excited to find the new Ice Palace location, bouncing on her feet in impatience. When he was at the bottom of the stairs, she pointed up. He looked and found a small blue dragon with orange flames on the ceiling several meters in front of him.

Kole kept his eyes on the girl and the dragons as they made their way deeper into the underground corridors. These looked much like the hallways at the last location, designed for utility access and maintenance. Not heavily trafficked based on the amount of dust accumulated along the sides, but the central pathway had been recently cleaned. No sense in scaring away customers who might think they'd found the wrong place.

After half a dozen turns, Neela came to a stop in front of a set of double doors. This time, Kole looked up and found the dragon marker just overhead. He noticed the head of the dragon was pointed down, the flames shooting out toward the door. He'd noticed earlier that the orientation of the markers indicated when to make a turn, based on the direction of the flames.

He put out an arm to stop the teenager before she could rush through the doors, and put a palm against the handle. It was cold to the touch. "Okay," he said in a near whisper, "we're going in slow. No rushing in, no loud noises. Keep your eyes and ears open, yeah?"

"Yeah, man. Okay. Can we go in?"

Kole grabbed her upper arms, turning her to face him and staring at her until her constantly moving eyes settled on his. "Neela, I want you to listen to me. You may think you know this Cady woman, but I promise you there is something going on here that is deeper than you realize. She's not a simple owner of an amusing bar with attractions for people like you."

Her lips tightened, but her gaze stayed on his. "I hear you. Not sure why you think so, like, but I'll be careful and cool, yeah?"

He had to take what he could get. As soon as he released her, Neela pushed the doors open and stepped inside the vast chamber beyond. It was easily twice the size of the previous location, and a dozen men and women were spraying water to form the skate rink and sled course. The bar was nothing more than a bunch of ice blocks that were being slowly chiseled into shape.

"We're not open yet," a voice said from out of view. "Come back tomorrow."

Cady appeared from where she'd been overseeing the work, an area of the room blocked from view by the open doors. She came to an abrupt stop when she saw them, the smile on her face slipping for half a second. Kole knew in that moment she was the one responsible for the attempt to breach *Rim Jumper*. She hid it well, though, continuing forward smoothly.

89

"Neela. Mr. Anwynn. It's a pleasure to see you both again. How did you ever find us again so quickly?"

"The dragons, man. Been looking all day, yeah?" Neela tried to contain her excitement, but her gaze was focused on the people shaping the sled run. She looked imploringly at Kole until he sighed and shrugged. "Can I?" she asked Cady.

"Go ahead," the woman said with an indulgent smile. As the teenager raced off to watch the work, Cady stood beside him. "And why exactly were you looking so hard for my club, bounty hunter?"

"I could ask why you moved it so abruptly after my last visit," he said, keeping his attention on the woman in case of any sudden movement. "Or why you were so eager to get into my ship when you found out I landed here."

One of her cheeks expanded, like she was rubbing her tongue against it. A nervous habit he'd noted in many people through the years. "If I told you I was just curious, would you believe me?"

"Nope," he said, with a hard glare. He noticed she had dropped the local inflection and slang, sticking to Galactic Standard quite proficiently.

"Didn't think so. Care to share another drink with me, Mr. Anwynn? I guess I have no choice but to tell you a story and hope you'll believe it."

She led him over to a door that opened onto a small storage closet behind where the bar would be. It was warmer inside, but still cold enough that he almost asked for the heavy coat he'd worn the last time he was in the Ice Palace. Cady pulled a bottle from an open crate, looked around fruitlessly for something to drink from, then tugged the cork from the top and took a deep pull. She passed the bottle over.

"I was contacted two days ago, by someone I've done a bit of work for in the past. The kind of person I'm far too afraid of to ask their name, and I'm sure you'll understand why. They told me that a bounty hunter was coming to Hebat Prime and described your ship down to the last detail. I was to have my contacts at the spaceport watch for you and send an alert upon your arrival.

"This person didn't ask me to break into your ship, but I couldn't stop wondering why they were so concerned about your arrival on Prime. You being a bounty hunter and all, I thought perhaps there was a juicy reward somewhere I could get in on. I wanted to find out what was on your server, but my techs assured me they couldn't access it without a bit of code manually installed from inside the ship.

"I made the mistake of hiring a couple of sleaze balls who frequent the Palace. All they had to do was get onto your ship, insert a data chip that would automatically load the code into your systems, and get out. Easiest credits of their lives."

She sighed and took the bottle back from him to drink deeply from the smooth liquor. It was clearly a top shelf bottle, the kind that few patrons to the establishment would be willing or able to afford. "They were supposed to wait for one of my shipyard contacts to arrive and help them get past your ship's defenses. Not rush in like idiots and get shot at."

"It wouldn't have helped," Kole said, taking a drink from the bottle that was passed back to him. "*Rim Jumper* has one of the best security systems available for a ship her size."

"As I found out," Cady murmured with a grimace. "And then you killed one of the idiots, and the other came running to me only minutes ahead of the security forces who were bound to be chasing him. Damned fool could have brought them down on all our heads."

Kole wasn't surprised the man hadn't stuck around to be found lying on top of his dead partner. He almost pointed out that his ship had done the killing, but didn't bother. He would have gladly done it himself, given half the chance. "And then you killed him to save yourself."

"What would you have done, bounty hunter?" Cady looked at him with angry eyes. "I couldn't risk him talking when the security forces finally caught up to him, ruining everything I've built here."

"Tell me about this person that hired you. What do you know about them?"

"Almost nothing," she said, waving a hand through the air. She swayed with the movement, and he could tell the alcohol was starting to get to her. She'd drunk nearly half the bottle herself. "It's the third time they've hired me, but the others were just standard information gathering on locals."

"How did they contact you? Are they male? Female?"

"Anonymous messages through the planetary network, so I have no idea on gender. I had one of my techs run a trace on the first message, but it bounced across seven different systems before it was lost completely."

"Once you told them I'd arrived, what happened? Did they ask you to do anything else?"

"Yes," she said miserably, slumping down to sit on an unopened crate. "They told me to follow you, and report anyone you spoke with for more than a few minutes."

"No one has been following me," Kole said with a sniff. "I'm good enough to pick up on that."

"Didn't have to follow you," Cady said, gulping down a large drink. "I paid someone who was already in contact with you and knew every move you've made since you landed."

He stiffened, closing his eyes as he felt the betrayal set in. The person he'd trusted most on Prime, opened up to more than he ever did with anyone. She was the perfect spy, and probably didn't even realize she was being used.

CHAPTER TWELVE

He found Neela jabbering away at a couple of the people spraying water to add sloped sides to the sled course. She was her normal barely contained ball of excitement, and as he walked toward her, he saw her looking around for a sled she could grab to get on the course before it was ready.

The young woman saw him coming halfway across the chamber, waving at him with a wide smile. His own neutral expression didn't even make her pause as she turned back to the people she was talking to.

Cady had told him how she'd paid the girl to make sure her taxi was available when he left the spaceport. Neela received ten credits just to send a message each time Kole stopped the taxi to speak with someone. An extra ten credits if Neela could supply any details about what he might have seen that person about. It was Cady who talked the girl into sticking with him throughout the day. Apparently, the desire to stay with him a second day had been purely her own.

"If you make the sides tall, like, we can try to do a loop. That be fun, yeah? Maybe even two loops!"

Kole wrapped his fingers around her wrist, pulling her roughly away from the others. She let out a startled yelp but followed along compliantly enough. "What's up, man? You get the information you wanted?"

94

"I found out that someone has been reporting my every move," he said quietly.

Neela blushed, having the grace to look away. "Yeah, I meant to tell you about that. It was just for credits, like, and just to Cady. She's not dangerous or anything."

"You are going to have to grow up someday," he said, knowing his voice was harsher than it needed to be. "Your friend Cady is the boss of a little criminal organization operating out of the Ice Palace. She's been giving all the information you pass to her to the person that wants me dead."

Her eyes had gone wide, mouth dropping open with surprise. "No, man. Cady never do that to me, like. Never!"

Kole turned to the storage closet, where the woman was leaning against the doorframe draining the last of the bottle. She was drinking to assuage her own guilt over using the girl, but it didn't make him feel any better about her. "She did it, Neela. For the same reason most people do things, because she was paid quite well for it."

"No, man. No." Neela was rocking back and forth now, still trying to wrap her head around the betrayal of a woman she'd thought of as a friend for so many years. Despite her age and her ability to fend for herself, she was incredibly naïve. Kole had to admit it was one of the traits that had made him feel so attached to her. She needed to be protected from the people in the universe who would use that naivety against her.

Cady had told him something else in the storage closet, something that he felt confident would get him one step closer to the person who attacked his ship. He couldn't do anything with that information until he got back to the spaceport, though.

Neela's eyes were watering, and he reached out to put an arm around her shoulders and pull her close. She buried her face in his chest and started to shake with sobs. "I'm sorry, man. I didn't mean to hurt you, yeah? Never want that."

"I know," he said soothingly, glaring at the workers who looked over curiously. They found much more interesting things to look at in other directions. The teenager kept repeating apologies, but he stayed silent and just held her. The anger he'd felt at the betrayal had dissipated at the first sign of her horrified realization.

Neela finally pulled away, rubbing a sleeve across her eyes and nose. She couldn't meet his eyes, and it almost hurt to see how depressed she was. "Look, I'm not mad at you. I just want you to realize that your actions do have consequences. You have to learn to think things through, alright? Not everyone is as nice and good as you are."

She mumbled something, too quietly to hear. Then she leaned forward and hurried over to the double doors to pull one open just wide enough to squeeze through. Kole sighed, thinking he might have to look for another taxi back to the spaceport. He couldn't blame the teenager if she decided she didn't want to be his driver anymore.

He stopped at the double doors to stare over at Cady. She met his eyes defiantly, but he could tell from her inability to even lean against the wall without swaying that she was going to be out of it shortly. It took all his willpower to keep from sticking a knife through her deceitful mouth for what she'd done to Neela.

Kole yanked the door open and stomped out into the corridor. He was able to follow the dragon markers this time, winding his way through the underground tunnels until he found the stairs leading up to street level. The steel doors were still wide open, and he paused to pull them shut. Then he pushed through the screen of plant fronds.

Pink dreadlocks drew his attention to where Neela was sitting only a few meters away. She didn't look up as he fell onto the bench beside her. "If you want your credits back, like, I understand."

"I'd like it if you'd still help me. You can earn them."

"For reals, man? You still want me to drive you around Prime?"

He shrugged, waving at the hovercars that passed in the street not far away. "Who else is going to navigate all this? You just have to promise that I'm the only one you're sharing information with going forward."

"Yeah, man! Only you. I swear on everything, like." She was starting to smile again.

"Then let's go. I need to get back to the spaceport. There's some research I need to do before I decide on the next move."

Neela jumped up and led the way back to where the pink taxi had been parked. She almost ran circles around him the entire way, talking about how happy she was that he'd forgiven her. Promising that she wouldn't give information to anyone else ever again. Kole expected that she'd learned something, and only hoped that his unknown assassin hadn't gotten too much of a leg up on him with everything she'd passed along already. At least he now knew why they'd never returned his message about the fabricated contract.

Once back at the spaceport he stopped at the security forces station. They were able to direct him to the administrative offices. Getting in proved a bit more difficult, with a security reader on the door that blocked access to all but the people who worked within. Kole found a comfortable spot to wait, and he leaned against a wall to watch everyone who approached the door or exited from within.

Cady had told him about her contact in the spaceport office, a young man who had racked up a large gambling debt at another of her businesses. She offered him the option of paying it off with information, and the idiot hadn't bothered to ask for set terms on the exchange. She'd be milking him for the rest of his career.

The man she'd described finally appeared from within the administrative offices, walking toward the nearest food court with his face buried in his datapad screen as he walked. Kole was breathing down his neck before he realized someone else was there, and he turned with an angry look.

"Do you mind?"

"Not at all," Kole said with a small smile. "Derrick."

That made the man stop in his tracks. "How do you know my name?"

"We have a mutual friend. She told me that you're the man with all the information around here."

Derrick swallowed, the prominent lump in his throat rising and falling. "I don't know what you mean, sir. If you'll excuse me." He turned away, walking quickly back in the direction of the offices.

Kole put a hand on his shoulder, bringing him to a halt. "No reason to make this messy, huh? All I want to know is if you've ever seen a small ship land on this planet. It's no larger than twice the size of a life pod."

He went pale, and his lips started trembling. "That... but... you don't want to know about that ship. I promise you."

"And I promise that I do." Kole squeezed the man's shoulder, eliciting a wince of pain.

Derrick swallowed again, his tongue poking out to lick dry lips. "Do you know how much trouble I could get in if anyone knew I was even talking about that ship?"

Kole sighed, put on his most feral smile, and leaned in close. "Do you know how much trouble you could get in if you *don't* tell me about it?"

The young man was trembling now, and Kole worried he might collapse. There was a large planter nearby with a small tree in it, the lip large enough to sit on. He guided Derrick over to get him off his feet, then sat near him and looked around to make sure they weren't drawing unwanted attention.

"Look, the person that uses that ship is not someone you want to protect. If you give me any information on how I can find it, I can guarantee they'll never bother you again."

"How can you do that? The only way they wouldn't come after me is if they're dead." Kole stared at him for half a minute, until he saw understanding dawn in the frightened eyes. "You're going to… you think you can do that?" It was asked with an almost hopeful tone.

"I know that I can, if I find them before they find me."

Derrick's eyes darted around wildly, as he tried to work out the best course of action. The one that would give him the least amount of risk. Kole gave him a few moments, and then added a sweetener to the pot. "If you tell me where to find that ship, and I put an end to whoever is a threat to both of us, I'll also get Cady to release your debt."

"You can do that?"

"She owes me. I think she'll be quite happy to get off so easily."

Derrick shot to his feet and almost ran back to the door into the administrative offices. He moved faster than Kole had expected, and he was barely on his feet before the man was swiping his palm over the reader and pulling the door open. Kole sank back onto the rim of the planter, hoping he wasn't going to be visited by security guards soon.

Five very tense minutes later, Derrick reappeared. He was carrying a small data chip pinched between two fingers, which he held out as he approached. "The information is on here.

Make sure you scrub whatever drive you use it on. I don't want any trace left behind that could get back to me if you fail."

"I won't fail," Kole said with a hard smile as he took the chip. "You shouldn't hear from Cady again." He walked away, ignoring the man's attempts to obtain assurances.

CHAPTER THIRTEEN

In the cockpit of *Rim Jumper*, Kole pushed the data chip into a slot on one of his displays. A file pulled up, showing arrivals and departures for a small ship over the last year. It was listed as the *Gazelle*, a single passenger ship. No other details. It had left Hebat Prime five times in the last Galactic Standard year, always returning after no less than ten days.

"ShANN, any chance we can correlate these dates with assassinations that have occurred throughout the Rim?"

Her face shimmered into view over the holograph projector. "You are assuming your quarry only operates in the Rim, Captain Anwynn. I would also point out that the best assassins make their kills look accidental. Much as yours would have appeared, should the sneak attack have succeeded."

He waved a hand through the air. "I know I'm grasping at straws here, but run it anyway. Maybe we'll get lucky."

"Very well," she said. If he didn't know better, he'd say her face looked disapproving as it faded away.

He swiped the display, pulling up another document. This showed the departure and arrival vectors for the ship. It never landed at the main spaceport, so he plotted the trajectories to see if he could determine where the ship was docking. Unfortunately, the ship was too small for the sensors to pick it up easily. The data provided was spotty at best, and the ship seemed to almost be invisible within a couple of kilometers of the planet's surface.

Kole was able to narrow it down to four of the estates on the northern edge of the energy barrier that protected Prime from the system's supersized sun. They were the only other places to land a ship aside from the spaceport, unless someone were stupid enough to set down outside the protective barrier and try to walk in unprotected. The solar radiation was strong enough to cook a human body within three hours, and anyone exposed to the sun for more than fifteen minutes would be suffering ill effects for the rest of their lives.

While he waited on results from ShANN's search, he checked on the protective gear worn by the workers who serviced and installed the solar spikes across the planet. Most of the work was done by remote-controlled drones, while the operator was safe inside a heavily shielded shuttle. But there were times that a hands-on approach was called for. In those instances, the workers had to put on heavy suits with about fifty layers of various materials that could absorb or deflect radiation before it reached skin and muscle.

Those suits were incredibly expensive, too. Kole found a handful of shops across Prime selling them, but the cheapest was fifteen hundred credits. More than most citizens of the planet would earn in a month. The sales were also reported to the planetary governor's office and the security forces. They didn't want some unknown psycho running around the surface of the planet and possibly harming the precious solar spikes that provided more than ninety percent of the system's income.

Kole made a mental note of that, thinking he could find a way to get the information from the government's databases if it came down to that. There was always someone willing to sell information for a couple hundred credits. He would check the four estates first, though, and see if he could gain access to any docking facilities on them.

ShANN's face reappeared while he was looking at satellite maps of those areas. "Captain Anwynn, the results of my search have been too varied to allow for any correlation between known facts. As I expected."

"In other words, no dice."

"I'm sorry, captain. Was I supposed to include dice in the search parameters?"

He groaned and shook his head. "Old expression, ShANN. Can you look at these entry and exit vectors? I think that ship has to be docking in one of four places, but maybe you can tighten my search area a little."

The hologram flickered for a second as she processed the information. "Your estimated source for the ship is correct, Captain Anwynn. However, the data would point toward the Welkins estate as being the most probable."

Kole zoomed in on that location on the satellite map. It was hard to see anything under the energy barrier, which all looked like a heavily out of focus image, but he could see a slight bulge in the shielding that seemed to be extending to cover what could be a landing site. He wished he had access to recorded images from the satellites instead of just the public access stills that were released months apart.

"That's as good a place to start as any. Thanks, ShANN."

Now he just had to figure out how to get onto the estate. At least getting there wouldn't be too much of a problem.

The pink taxi was still parked at the curb when he exited the spaceport. Neela was sitting on the hood, arguing with an exhausted tourist who was holding out a ten-credit chip begging her to take him to his hotel. The line of people waiting for the other taxis was long enough that Kole couldn't blame him.

"Sorry, man. I got a customer, yeah, and he isn't you." She spotted Kole and jumped down with a happy grin. "This him. You want to keep arguing?"

The tourist grumbled but walked away after a glance at the bounty hunter. The young woman hurried around the hovercar to hold the door open as Kole approached, and he raised an eyebrow. "Number one customer service," she told him with a grin.

She pulled into traffic in her normal reckless manner, then turned back to look at him eagerly. "Where to, man? You find something good?"

"How close can we get to one of the estates on the northern edge of the city?"

Neela sniffed, looking at him as if expecting a punch line. "You serious, like? Why would you want to go there?"

"Because I think the person I'm looking for is keeping their ship in one of the estate's private docking facilities. Maybe they even live there."

105

"No way someone like us get onto an estate, man. You got to have tons of credits, like. Or know the right people."

"Let's just see how close we can get, okay? The Welkins estate. Do you know which one that is?"

She gave him the kind of look every teenager perfected, clearly expressing that he should have known better than to think he had to ask. Then she twisted around to put her attention back on the road and yanked the wheel to get them back into the middle of the lane.

Kole settled in for the ride. The estates were on almost the opposite side of Prime, and they'd have to go through the dense traffic of the city center or all the way around the outskirts. Neela, never one for soft approaches, headed straight through Prime.

An hour and a half later, the car was passing through an area of the city with widely spaced buildings. All of them were four to six stories, an ostentatious show of low-level wealth on a world where space was at a premium. He briefly wondered how long it would be before the population grew to a point where these smaller buildings would have to be torn down and replaced with towering structures capable of providing housing for thousands.

Before the road came to an end at an elaborate gate in the distance, Neela pulled into a parking lot, gawking at the empty stretch of concrete set aside for nothing but hovercars. To someone who was born and grew up in the dense urban area, it boggled the mind to think that even a dozen meters of ground had been set aside solely for parking vehicles.

106

Kole leaned forward, looking through the windscreen at the black steel gates that protected the estate ahead of them. The bars of the gate and fence were thick, but there was enough of a gap between them to make out stretches of green grass ahead. He couldn't see any sign of a house.

"Are these estates just gardens?"

She laughed. "No, man. Big, big houses way back, like. Got to drive for five minutes or more to reach them, I heard."

"That means it's an absurdly large amount of land. No way they can have security watching every inch of it." He looked at the gate access mechanism, a hand scanner that also included genetic sampling if he remembered the specs on that model. Not the sort of thing that could be easily bypassed, and also in an exposed area that had to be under constant surveillance. "Are there any roads that travel along the fences around the estate?"

Neela twisted her lips to the side and made a humming sound. She tapped the small computer screen on her dash, waking the system and pulling up a navigations system. Her fingers moved across it quickly as she scanned the map, looking at all the road systems around this part of Prime. "No way, man. The snobs be paranoid, yeah? Big riots in the way, way back, and the richies had to protect themselves from the reekers."

Kole thought that meant the wealthy elite were afraid of the poorer citizens ganging up and running rampant. It had happened thousands of times in the past, across thousands of systems. A planet on the Rim that had been settled for more than a couple of centuries, Hebat Prime was long due for that kind of social upheaval. Especially with so much wealth concentrated in so few hands.

"I guess we get a little exercise then," he said, pushing the passenger door open and standing up to stretch in the parking lot. It felt good to be in such a wide-open space, something he'd grown used to in his travels around the Rim. Few settled worlds were as tightly contained as Prime.

Neela looked around at all the open-aired space with suspicion. He almost laughed at how tense she appeared, like she expected something to jump out at any moment. He glanced at her hair for a moment and clicked his tongue. "Do you have anything to hide the dreads, Neela?"

"What's wrong with my dreads, man?" She gave him an angry pout.

"I love them, I really do. But I don't think they quite fit in for this part of Prime. Yeah?"

She raised one of the pink strands of hair, looking at it and shrugging. "Could be right, like." She ducked back into the car, digging around for a bit before pulling out a large pullover with an attached hood. It swamped the petite girl, the sleeves falling past her fingers. But the hood covered her hair and made her stand out less. "Peter left it, like, and I didn't feel like tracking the loser down to return it."

Kole guessed Peter was a prior boyfriend but didn't care enough to ask. He tugged the shoulders of the pullover straight and tried to knot the edges of the hood to keep it from covering her eyes too much. "Good enough," he said finally.

He led her away from the parking lot, walking as casually as possible as they left the sidewalk and crossed into the grass. They walked parallel to the fence around the estate, trying to stay far enough from the steel bars to not draw attention. Most security systems Kole had encountered in his career didn't extend far beyond the edge of the protected area, especially away from any entry points.

"How long we going to walk, man?" Neela was already dragging after less than half a kilometer.

"Until I see what I'm looking for," he said. "You can wait by the car if you'd like."

"I'm coming with you, like. You get in trouble when I'm not around." Kole snorted a laugh. The way he remembered it was that he got in trouble because of her, but he let it go.

They continued along the fence for five kilometers. He didn't find a single place where the fence looked weaker than in other sections. Whoever was maintaining the security for the estates was doing a stellar job. Unfortunately for him.

As soon as he came to a halt, the teenager dropped down to sit on the yellowish-green grass. She was breathing hard, too unaccustomed to walking such long distances. While Kole examined the fence line, she fell onto her back and looked up at the shimmering energy field high above.

"Be so much easier if we were up there, yeah? Could see *over* the fence, like."

He looked up with her, spotting a glider far overhead. Spacecraft weren't allowed inside the barrier, but he hadn't thought to look into the possibility of other airborne vehicles. "Do you know anyone who could get us up there?"

She grinned at him. "I know a guy, man. Going to cost you a lot of credits, like."

CHAPTER FOURTEEN

"Two hundred credits for an hour of flight time."

Kole narrowed his eyes, examining the wiry man rubbing his hands with a grease-stained cloth. After walking back to the taxi, with Neela complaining about the distance almost the entire time, they had driven to a small hanger on the edge of an airfield situated near the center of the string of estates. There were only a handful of aircraft arrayed inside, small gliders with ancient piston engine design.

"I can't get you over one of the estates, though," the pilot said with an unconcerned shrug. "Best I can do is flying along the property line."

"That's good enough for us, man." Neela was circling the small glider, running her hands over the thin material that covered the aircraft frame. "Just got to see, yeah."

The pilot looked between the two of them, pursing his lips. "Can't take you both. Too much weight for the glider."

Neela looked stricken at the words. She knew which of them would be making the trip in that case, and she'd be left on the ground to miss out on the fun.

"Three hundred credits," Kole said. "Two hours. You take me up first, then the girl second." The pilot nodded and started prepping the glider for the first trip.

"Thank you, thank you, thank you," Neela screeched as she ran over and threw her arms around Kole. He wasn't entirely sure how to deal with that, so he patted her once on the back and waited for her to let go. "You the best, man. The best!"

"I just want two opinions on what we see, that's all." It didn't dilute her unbridled joy. She took off to follow the pilot, watching intently as he checked over the glider and verified the charge on the batteries. He didn't seem perturbed in the least as she peppered him with questions, answering with grunts or single words.

It didn't take very long for the aircraft to be ready. Kole helped the pilot push it out of the hanger, amazed at how light the craft was. He barely had to exert any strength once it was rolling along the smooth tarmac. They pushed until it was just behind a set of three yellow lines, and then the pilot popped open the hatch on the seating compartments.

Kole sat behind the pilot, with a transparent canopy surrounding them to below his shoulder level. The pilot pushed a few switches, tapped on some gauges, and then pushed a button that started the loud engine. A five-bladed propeller on the nose of the craft began spinning, and the pilot pushed his control stick forward. The glider bounced along the tarmac as it built up speed, lifting from the ground just before the long runway ended.

"I'll get us up to half a kilometer, and then fly along the estate borders," the pilot said over his shoulder. Kole felt beads of sweat form on his forehead, and he couldn't believe he was putting his life in the hands of such ancient technology.

The glider circled a few times as it gained altitude, and then the pilot straightened the course. Kole looked out over the land spread beneath him. He could see the rising towers of Prime much closer than he would have expected. In the other direction was vast swathes of grassy emptiness. He could see large mansions in the distance, with the haze of the energy barrier seemingly falling right behind them.

They were able to make four passes along the edges of the estates in the hour given to him. On the second, Kole finally picked out the estate of the Welkins family. It was smaller than the two on either side, but still consisted of enough unused land to easily build a dozen or more large towers to provide homes and jobs for tens of thousands of citizens.

Trees lined the single road leading to the mansion. There were guard posts just inside the main gate, another pair halfway down the road, and then another set before a tall stone wall that seemed the surround the mansion grounds. A lot of security to keep the family feeling safe and protected.

"Do you get a lot of people who want to fly past the estates like this?"

"Oh yeah," the pilot said with a big nod. "People who get promoted into the lower ranks of management always want to come over and see how the richies live. They all think they'll be living like that someday." He waved a hand at the estate they were passing.

"What would happen if you flew over an estate boundary?"

"Don't even think about it, son. You may not be able to see them, but each estate has laser cannons with automatic firing systems. If I get within a few dozen meters of their boundaries, they paint my glider with laser targeting."

"Would you encroach on that border for an extra hundred credits?"

The pilot's head twisted as far as it could. "You got a death wish, son?"

"My only wish is to see these defenses for myself. You can veer out of the restricted zone quickly."

They flew in silence for a while, and Kole thought the pilot was going to just ignore the insane idea. "Two hundred," the pilot finally said.

"Done. Wait until I give the word to edge over the boundary line." Kole waited as the glider looped around to begin the fourth pass along the estates. Once he judged they were close to the Wilkens estate, he reached out and tapped the pilot's shoulder.

The glider jerked to the side, as if an errant air current had caught the wing. It strayed over the fence along the edges of the estate, and Kole watched with fascination as patches of grass halfway to the mansion slid aside to reveal a pair of large laser cannons. The same thing happened on the neighboring estates, sensing the violation. The cannons instantly zeroed in on the glider, a bright flash of the laser-assisted targeting system painting the aircraft.

"Don't shoot!" the pilot said urgently into his headset, talking with the estate's security team. "I'm correcting course now. It was an engine malfunction, that's all." He was silent, and Kole could hear a faint voice from the headset. "Yes, sir, I'm going to have the techs check my glider carefully. Sorry about that."

As the glider tilted to return to the original flight path, Kole kept his eyes on the laser cannons. They followed the glider until it passed over the boundary, then dropped below ground level again. Once the panels covered them, it was almost impossible to spot the location of each in the field of yellow-green grass.

The glider descended slowly, and the wheels screeched as they met the tarmac. It bounced even more as the brakes slowed their speed, until the craft was crawling along toward the hangar. "I know you wanted your daughter to have a ride, but I can't risk those security guards wondering why I'm back in the air so soon when I told them we had a malfunction."

"Not my daughter," Kole said. "I'm sure she'll understand."

Neela did not understand.

"What do you mean I can't go, man? You promised me I could fly, yeah?" She was almost in tears with her frustration and disappointment.

"I did, but it's not safe to go up right now." Kole raised his hands to stem her words. "I've talked to the pilot, and you can come back in a day or two. I've already paid for the ride."

She pouted but seemed slightly mollified. The pilot was grinning from ear to ear with an extra five hundred credits stuffed in his pockets to ensure the teenager could return and get a ride at any time. She looked back at the glider longingly as she followed Kole out of the hanger and back to the taxi.

"What now, man? You see something good, like?"

"Laser cannons," he said, thinking about the smudge he had seen behind the mansion. It was hard to tell from a distance, but it had looked like a building butted right up against the energy shield. The perfect place to store a small vessel that you wanted to keep hidden when it wasn't being used. He'd had the forethought to wear his video lens during the flight, so he pulled out his datapad to watch the feed and try to get an enhanced view.

"That don't sound good, Kole." Neela was twisted around in her seat, face almost mashed against the clear divider as she tried to see what he was doing on the computer. "How you get in if they shoot you?"

"We have to find a way in when they're not shooting," he said simply. He'd found the right portion of the recording, and he zoomed in on the area. Advancing the video slowly, he was able to pause it at a point where the view of the building was as clear as it could be from such a distance. It was larger than it had initially looked and appeared to be far beyond the large mansion. He couldn't tell from the angle, but he felt certain his guess about it being right up against the protective barrier was correct.

"When are they not shooting?" Neela asked, looking at the video upside down with furrowed brows.

"When they're expecting visitors," Kole said as he closed the video. "If there's one thing rich people love, it's having lavish parties and showing off how much money they have. We just need to find out when the next one is, and use it to get in."

"Yeah, man, I just put on my best dress and we stroll right through the gates," she said with an exaggerated eye roll.

"Something like that," he said with a smile.

CHAPTER FIFTEEN

As Neela drove back into the more populated regions of the city, Kole searched the local networks for any hint of upcoming parties on the estates. The best he could find was a charity gala being hosted by the Pendleton family. That estate was beside the Wilkens estate. Close enough that it could fit his purposes. He searched for how to get into the event, finding that anyone donating at least twenty thousand credits to the Pendleton's favorite charity received an invite.

It was a large amount of money, more than he made on most jobs he worked. Kole had to seriously consider whether he felt the danger justified the expenditure. In the end, it was Neela that decided it for him.

"So cool, man. Can you imagine being in with all the richies, like? Eating their food, drinking their booze, touching their stuff. Be the best night ever, yeah."

He told himself he sent the charitable donation because his pride wouldn't let him find a cheaper way to get a line on the assassin. Or because he could use it as an excuse to develop contacts among the wealthy families of Hebat Prime, who would undoubtedly need the services of someone like him at some point.

But he knew better.

As they were passing through the city core, Kole directed her to park near a string of shops. The windows were filled with clothing that looked respectable and expensive. Neela raised an eyebrow as they got out of the taxi. "You need a suit, like? Got to fit in with the richies?"

"No, I already have one. In my line of work, you never know where you'll need to fit in." He looked at her with a smirk. "But the invitation I've received allows me to bring a guest. And my guest is going to need to look her best."

Neela's mouth dropped open. "You mean it, Kole? I can go with you?"

"If you'd like to," he said as if it didn't matter to him one way or another.

"Don't be joking with me, like. You really taking me to the richie's party, man?"

In response, he waved at the shops in front of them. "You just have to get the right clothing to fit in."

She almost ran through the river of pedestrians between the curb and the shop entrances, pushing through the throng. Kole laughed and followed at a slower pace to squeeze through without causing as much of a disruption. By the time he caught up, she was already in the first shop running her fingers down a silky dress.

"It's so pretty," she said in a whisper.

A saleswoman approached with a sneer on her face, eyeing both of them and immediately pegging them as people who couldn't afford the goods on offer. "Can I help you?" *Find your way back outside,* the unspoken completion of the question.

Kole held up a hundred-credit chip. The frosty look instantly melted, and the saleswoman became all solicitousness as she helped Neela look through the clothing on offer and select a few dresses to try on. Kole leaned against the wall just inside the entrance, trying not to smile as the young woman babbled about the party she was going to attend.

"What you think, man?" she asked after exiting the changing room in the first dress. It was deep yellow, with white and red trim throughout. The pink dreadlocks presented a starkly disconcerting contrast with it, but ignoring them he had to admit she looked very good in the attire.

"It looks nice," he said.

She smiled at him, turning to disappear back into the dressing room. Over the next half hour, he saw her in a dozen dresses and pant suits. Some were stunning in the way they made her appear to be much older and less wild. Others were so horrendous he couldn't hold back the laughter as she presented herself in them with lips pressed tightly together to keep her own amusement from bursting out.

In the end, she chose a crimson dress that was cut in the latest fashion. There was a yellow silk wrap that was included, for her to throw over her shoulders in case she felt a chill in the dress that left far more skin uncovered than Kole had expected. For a moment, he understood how fathers could become so overprotective of their children.

He paid for the selection, carrying the bag containing the purchase as he followed Neela back onto the street. She started to head for the taxi, but he grabbed her wrist to stop her and turned in a different direction.

"What now, man? Got the fancy dress already."

"Now you need a little pampering." He led her along to a salon that he'd noted when they parked. A handful of women were seated in comfortably padded chairs throughout the room as they entered. A few looked up curiously, but most ignored them. Neela was looking around in bewilderment as an employee approached.

Five minutes later, the teenager was seated in a chair looking at herself in the mirror with wide eyes. "You can't take my dreads, man. They mine, like."

"We can get them back whenever you'd like," the man standing behind her said, with a wink at Kole. He then ran his hands through her hair, talking to her about the variety of stylings he thought would look best on her. Soon, Neela's reluctance was fading, helped in no small part by the small holographic display the stylist used to show her how she'd look with a few different cuts. They finally found one that had her bouncing in her seat with excitement.

Kole leaned his head back, feeling relaxed in the comfortable chair he was waiting in. At some point, his eyes drifted closed, and he must have fallen asleep. A touch on his arm jerked him awake, and he blinked as he looked around. The man who'd been working with Neela was standing in front of him, his white teeth showing in a wide smile.

"Your girlfriend is ready, sir, if you'd like to see."

"Not my girlfriend," Kole said as he stood. He followed to a curtained-off area at the rear of the salon. The stylist turned back to look at him before jerking the curtain open.

The woman sitting within was dazzling. Dark brown curls flowed to her shoulders, a sweep of hair half covering one sparkling eye. Kole sucked in a breath, stunned by the changes.

Neela was blushing, looking at him for his reaction. "Do I look okay, like?" She sounded very hesitant, as if afraid of what he'd say.

"You look fantastic," he said, being honest. "Hard to believe you're just a teenager."

A shadow crossed her face, and her mouth compressed. She looked away, mumbling something he couldn't hear. The stylist started talking about how she should care for her hair to keep it from frizzing up. While he covered all the tips, Kole swiped his finger across a pad to pay for the two hour visit. No wonder he'd fallen asleep in the chair.

She was still quiet as they left the salon and walked toward the taxi, subdued in a way he hadn't seen since she found out the information she'd been giving to Cady was being used against him. He was tempted to ask her what was wrong, but he decided not to be intrusive. Maybe it was just the loss of her beloved dreadlocks, and second thoughts about the change. There was no way she'd have been allowed onto the estate looking that way, though. He'd seen enough of the city in his two days to know they were a fashion choice among the younger and less affluent crowd.

Back in the taxi, he told her to head for the spaceport. He had preparations of his own to make. It was the quietest ride he'd been on since he first saw the pink taxi, which made him uncomfortable for some reason.

As they got close to their destination, he leaned forward to speak through the divider. "Is there a place you can park the hovercar for the evening? We're going to need to arrive at the estate in something more fitting for the occasion."

Neela looked even more sad at the words, and he realized how disparaging it might sound when she was so attached to the vehicle. Finally, she nodded, and turned off a short distance ahead to circle around the normal route. Soon they took another turn, dropping down a ramp into an underground parking area. Other taxis filled most of the space, waiting to be called in to pick up arriving tourists and visitors.

She carefully guided the taxi into an empty spot, with none of the exuberance he was accustomed to seeing when she drove. The hovercar settled to the ground, and the engines spun down into silence. They climbed out of the car, and as they walked away, he heard a loud chirp as the vehicle's locks were engaged.

Kole followed as Neela led him through the parking area, into a level of the spaceport he hadn't seen before. There were many more people than he was accustomed to seeing on the floor above, rushing to and fro as they hurried to get bags from trundling racks driven by low-level AI that tried to find owners of the luggage. Amongst them were locals trying to find their friends or family among the most recent arrivals.

Neela wove through them, her head down. She was walking purposefully, her new curls bouncing with each step. He
followed, still trying to figure out what had happened to cause
the recent change in her behavior. Had he not been as effusive
in his praise of the new hairstyle as he should have been?
Maybe she thought he didn't really like it.

He was about to speak and let her know that he liked the
way she looked even without the dreadlocks, but she suddenly
jogged forward. A lift was opening ahead, spilling out a dozen
people. The girl clambered inside as soon as it was empty,
putting an arm up to hold the door while he entered. Her eyes
didn't meet his.

The ride up to the next level was short, and as soon as the
doors opened, she was quick to exit. *Rim Jumper* was docked
far down the concourse, and they walked side by side through
the larger and emptier departures area. Kole remembered he
was carrying the bag with her new dress and passed it over.
"You can use the extra cabin on my ship to change. I'll make
arrangements for our transportation, and then we can leave
here in about three hours. Sound good?"

"Sure," she said, a flat answer that made him more worried
than anger would have. No local slang or rapid cadences, just
a single word.

As they passed through the security scanner and doors that
led to the landing pad, he pulled out his datapad and pressed
the button that activated the ramp. He was happy to see a spark
of interest in her eyes as they walked up into the ship. She

looked around the cargo bay, and he braced for the hundred and one questions he expected.

"Where's the cabin?" she asked instead, standing with her eyes on the ground and both hands wrapped around the handle of the bag. Kole guided her along the sloping corridor, stopping just before the cockpit and pressing the panel that opened the door of the spare cabin. He'd forgotten about the five crates that filled one corner, but there was still plenty of room for her to move around, and the washroom was clear.

"Do you want to eat something before you get changed? The galley is fully stocked."

"No," she said, looking around the room. Her face flushed, though he couldn't see any reason for it.

"Okay. If you change your mind, I'll be in the cockpit or my cabin." He pointed across the corridor. She nodded and then reached up to press the button that closed the door.

Kole sighed and walked into the cockpit. "ShANN, am I ever going to understand teenage girls?"

"I'm sorry, Captain Anwynn, I do not have enough data to answer that question."

"Yeah, that's how I feel, too." He pulled up a local network search, and quickly found a company that offered transportation options that were upscale enough for going to the party on the Pendleton estate. The prices for the evening were double what he'd expected, which he put down to a savvy business owner realizing the market would support it when so many people would want to present the best impression of themselves.

With transportation secured, he pulled the details on the alias he'd used to make the charitable donation. The last thing he needed was for his own name to show up on the guest list in case the assassin was invited or keeping an eye on the estate neighboring the location where their ship was stored.

He groaned as he looked at the screen. He'd forgotten how extreme he had gone when setting up this identity. It was going to take a little longer to get ready than he'd expected.

CHAPTER SIXTEEN

When Neela entered the galley at the end of the three hours, Kole had to remind himself to breathe. Her newly curly hair was pulled back from her face, and the dress hugged her figure closer than he'd noticed earlier in the day. He coughed and turned away to cover his embarrassment at staring, running some water into his glass and slowly sipping it as he faced the wall.

He turned around once he was done and found the girl only a few steps away. She was looking at him with her head tilted to one side, confusion across her features. Her lips were pulled back in the beginning stages of a smile. *At least she's not mad at me anymore,* he thought.

Then he remembered what his face looked like. The partner he'd worked with when he started out had often harped on how the smallest changes were the best disguises. Kole must have been drunk when he designed this alias, and he felt even more stupid for not remembering that when he chose it for the charitable donation. Two large moles stood out on his left cheek, several black hairs tufting out of one as if it had been a few days since they were trimmed. Wrinkles covered his forehead and surrounded his mouth, and his hair had been whitened with a solution that would last through the night.

"Grandpa," she said, reaching out to touch the moles but pulling her hand back before making contact.

127

"What do you think? Will anyone know it's me?"

"I'm still not convinced it's you," she said, unable to look away from the moles. Precisely the reason he'd chosen them in his inebriated state.

Kole noticed the lack of local slang, and the way her voice had dropped a few octaves. She was speaking slower, almost matching his own Outer Core accent. It was really quite impressive from someone who wasn't used to mimicking others.

He held out an arm, and she draped her hand through his elbow. "Our transport awaits." They left *Rim Jumper*, and he activated the ship's defenses. If anyone happened to discover he was going to the gala, it would be the perfect chance to try penetrating his ship again.

Walking through the spaceport, they drew quite a few stares. He wasn't sure if it was because of the fancy attire, or his own slightly hideous looks. He was wearing an expensive and custom-tailored suit. The cut might not be as impressive according to local fashion, but through much of the Rim he often drew compliments when he attended events in it.

Of course, the attention could just as easily have been drawn to Neela, who looked absolutely gorgeous. Had he seen the young woman across the spaceport, he would have certainly given her a second glance. It was hard not to keep turning his head to look at her, as it was.

"You look great, by the way." He tried to say the words casually, not putting too much emphasis on anything. When he glanced over, he saw her looking up at him with the first smile he'd seen in too long.

A long black car was waiting just outside the spaceport. Kole presented himself to the driver, swiping a thumb over the scanner to verify his identity. A patch of skin with the alias fingerprint and biometric readings had taken ten minutes to apply and blend in with his skin.

The driver was quick to open the door for them, holding out a hand to help Neela into the vehicle. Kole was glad to see that she acted as though the gesture were something she dealt with often. He wondered if she'd seen it in entertainment videos and was copying those motions.

Once inside the hovercar, he realized why the cost had been so much more than expected. It was one of the nicest vehicles he'd ever been in, and the wine bar against the divider that gave them privacy was fully stocked. With some of the best vintages, he noted as he looked over the labels. He pulled one bottle out, remembering how much he'd enjoyed it years before when it had been offered by a wealthy client during a celebration of a successful job.

"Are you going to open that, or just drool over it?"

He looked at Neela, returning her grin. "I didn't want to enjoy it when you can't have any."

"Oh? Why can't I?"

"Surely Hebat Prime has laws about legal drinking ages?"

Her smiled faded, replaced by a pouting frown. "You really do think I'm just a kid, don't you?"

That flustered him, a feeling he was unaccustomed to. "Well, aren't you?"

She sighed, crossing her arms over her chest and turning to look straight ahead. He had to congratulate himself on getting her upset with him again in record time. At least this time he thought he knew why she was angry, though he still didn't fully understand. Was the drinking age on Prime in the teenage years? Or did she just want people to think she was older than she looked?

Whatever the case, it wasn't the time to solve it. Kole popped the cork on the wine and grabbed two glasses. He filled both with a small amount of wine, then handed one to Neela. Even if she was underage, he didn't really care about drinking laws. As long as she was responsible, she could make her own decisions.

They sipped the drinks, and Kole kept waiting for her to start in on questions about the party. She'd been so excited when she found out he was taking her, yet now she was acting as if it were just another night in the social circuit. Any more of this, and he'd have to wonder what kind of actress he'd gotten involved with.

"When we arrive, just follow my lead," he said, after half an hour with no questions. "People like these are used to vapid party chatter, so they'll never ask anything too intrusive. Great job on the accent and dropping of the slang, too. I'm impressed."

That earned him a slight smile. "I didn't grow up on the streets, you know. I just learned to fit in when it became necessary. Man." She poked her tongue out after the last word.

He was intrigued by that and wondered what kind of story was behind the change in circumstances hinted at. If her parents had important enough jobs to live in the middle sections of a tower, why would she be driving a taxi around the city? And why hadn't he considered that until this moment?

"I'm twenty-two, by the way."

Kole jerked his head around to look at her. Neela was staring at the divider, trying to act as if she didn't care how he reacted. He was totally shocked by the admission and berated himself for falling into assumptions without any kind of facts to back them up. "Really? I just assumed... I mean, you act so young."

"And you act like an ass, sometimes. Doesn't mean you are one, though, does it?"

He snorted at that. "Fair enough. I apologize for taking half a dozen years off your actual age." His eyes started to wander down to examine her dress again, and he forced himself to look away. *Keep your mind on business.*

"Everyone always thinks it," she admitted ruefully. "You don't want to know how many people ask me if I'm old enough to drive before they'll even get in my taxi."

"Well, it's better than the other way around, right? They could be asking to see your senior citizen card all the time."

Neela laughed at that, and he felt mostly forgiven for his faulty assumptions. Soon, she was telling him stories about situations she'd been in because of how young she looked, and they were both laughing over them. *How young she used to look*, he told himself, remembering how she definitely looked like a young woman in her twenties once she got into the dress without the dreadlocks that made her seem even younger than her face would lead you to believe.

Thinking about his own assumptions based off experiences seen on other worlds made something click in his brain. The assassin hired to kill him would be reacting to his actions based on their own encounters. If they were native to Hebat Prime, then those experiences would be driven by life on this world. There had to be a way he could use that to lure them into acting rashly. He made a mental note to talk to Neela about it after the party.

The car slowed as it approached the gate at the entrance to the estate. The window beside Kole lowered, and a guard stepped forward to lean down and look inside the vehicle. "Welcome to the Pendleton Estate," he said, his eyes travelling between them. "May I confirm your identity, please?"

Kole held out the thumb with the skin graft, and the guard ran a laser scanner over it. Within a couple of seconds, the machine beeped. "Thank you, Mr. Bodgston. Enjoy your evening." He heard the sound of the gate opening as the window closed, and then the car accelerated smoothly down the drive.

"Bodgston?" Neela asked, her nose crinkled with distaste.

"Old client. I figured if I were going to usurp someone's identity, it couldn't happen to a nicer guy than him."

"Is that where you got the idea for…" She twirled her finger over her own cheek, indicating the location of the moles on his own.

132

"No, that was inspired by a few too many glasses of vodka on Ruskva VIIII. It was funny at the time," he said with a shrug.

"Oh, it's still funny," she assured him with a smile.

With the touch of a button, the divider between their compartment and the driver became transparent. They watched in fascination as the car joined the line of vehicles waiting to drop off party attendees. The men and women alighting from them were dressed to impress, but almost all had serious expressions that spoke of a desire to not be seen having too much fun.

When it was their turn, Kole exited the car from his side while the driver hurried around to open the door and present a hand for Neela to use as she climbed out. Then she settled her yellow wrap around her shoulders, fussing with it until Kole had hobbled around so she could take his arm. He was careful to use slow steps, demonstrating the extreme caution used by those who had aged beyond the ability of rejuvenation treatments to keep their bodies looking young.

It took an eternity to climb the twenty broad stairs to the entrance of the mansion, and three other arriving couples passed them by with looks of disdain or pity. He noticed the latter were cast more in Neela's direction than his own. They paused outside the door, and Kole glanced at his companion to make sure she was ready for this.

CHAPTER SEVENTEEN

The foyer of the Pendleton mansion was larger than *Rim Jumper*'s cargo bay. A dozen liveried staff lined the walls on either side of the room, attentive for the slightest sign that a guest might require something. There were thirty of forty of those guests milling around, greeting friends or new faces before moving on to the other rooms of the house open to the party. Servers carrying trays with drinks and food weaved through it all, with a grace that had to be admired.

Kole picked up two glasses of sparkling wine from one tray, handing a glass to Neela. "Sip slowly," he said in a near whisper. She gave him a wink, holding the glass to her lips for a second. The level of liquid hadn't changed when she pulled it away, and he nodded in approval.

"What now, man?" she asked in a whisper. "You need to get over the fence, like, yeah?"

He grinned at the return of the slang, spoken when she knew it wouldn't be overheard. "I do, but we need to be seen first. In half an hour or so, I can disappear, and people will assume the old fart wore himself out and needs a nap."

"As they're prone to do," she said, rubbing a finger over his snowy locks. "Especially when they're trying to keep up with their obscenely young girlfriends." He choked on the small sip he was taking, coughing to clear his throat as she laughed. "You know they're all thinking it," she said with a

134

smirk. And it was true. He'd seen it in the eyes of the guard at the gate, and those outside the mansion. The guests in the foyer had that same knowing look in their eyes when they glanced at the pair.

"Sure, but they could also assume you're my granddaughter."

"*Great-great*-granddaughter," she said with a sniff.

He decided she was taking far too much enjoyment from poking fun at his apparent age, and he started to hobble through the room. She pulled her arm from the crook of his elbow, following along as if bored with the excruciatingly slow progress.

"Well, aren't you two just darling," a woman said as she hurried over to greet them. "I'm Melinsa Hammon. I don't believe we've met."

"Hector Bodgston," he said in a croaking voice. "This is…"

"I'm Natali Montoya," Neela said, reaching out to touch fingers with the woman.

"So nice to meet you. Are you two… a couple?" The woman raised her eyebrows with the question, obviously fishing for gossip she could share with all her friends at the party.

"Madly in love," Neela said, putting an arm over Kole's slumped shoulders. "Hector found me on the street one day, swept me off my feet, and we've been together ever since." She smiled widely, leaning her head against his shoulder.

Melinsa took it all in with glee. "Isn't that nice? It's always good to see people who don't let age stand in the way."

Then she hurried off, drawing close to several other women not far away.

"How was that?" Neela asked in joyful whisper.

"Don't lay it on so strong," Kole said, but he couldn't hide his admiration of her quick thinking. They continued through the room, stopping to chat with various people. Most weren't as open with their curiosity about the pair, but word quickly flew through the room that they were a couple and not relations. The men they spoke to were often smirking in good humor, while many of the women gave him disapproving glances.

Beyond the foyer, the party stretched along a hall with a long dining room on one side and a ballroom on the other. More food was laid out on the table in the dining room, and knots of guests stood around the room eating and talking. Neela grabbed his hand and dragged him into the room as soon as she saw it. Her eyes had gone wide with the old excitement.

"Is that *real* fish, like?" she asked as they stopped in front of a platter piled with crustaceans in purple shells.

"It is," he said. "Looks like a crab species from the oceans of Polynia II. Must have cost a fortune to ship them here."

"A fortune that wants to be in my belly," she said as she grabbed a plate from a stack, and then tried to figure out how to use the tongs to grab one of the crustaceans. Her tongue poked out in concentration, and she almost shrieked with joy when she managed to snare one and get it onto her plate. She looked around in embarrassment when she remembered where she was. "Want one, man?"

136

"No, thank you." He noticed her accent dropped into the street cant when she was excited. Something he'd have to warn her about before it drew unwanted attention. He followed slowly as she walked along the table and piled her plate with all the delicacies and dishes that were impossible to find beyond the borders of an estate. It was a meal that would have cost close to a thousand credits in a restaurant, if the establishment could have obtained the necessary ingredients.

"Do you think they eat like this every day?" she asked, as she bit into a delicate pastry stuffed with mushrooms that could never have been grown on Hebat Prime.

"I'm sure they do," he murmured, his eyes taking in all the people filling the room. He kept hoping to see something that would point out a possible assassin, but he knew such a person would be skilled at blending in. "There are worlds where everyone eats like this, even out here on the Rim."

"For true?" she said. "I want to live in a place like that someday."

"There are pros and cons to every world," he said distractedly, watching a group of two men and three women in one dark corner. They seemed to have selected an area that wasn't easy to observe, and where they could effortlessly spot anyone trying to eavesdrop. "For instance, Hebat Prime offers little livable space and yet the people I have met here are among the most vibrant and alive. You take joy in simple things, and don't yearn overly much for things you'll likely never have."

When she was quiet, he glanced over to see her staring at him with her head tilted to the side again. He was getting a

137

feeling that was the stance she took when she was studying something she couldn't fully understand.

"You get that from meeting me, Cady, and Pulsar?"

"You, mostly." He smiled at the thought of anyone thinking the two criminal bosses could take joy in simple things. "And from them," he said, motioning at the servers walking through the room. "Look at how they smile at everyone, and the way their eyes dart around taking in everything. On most planets, they would be disgruntled at having to do a job they see as beneath them, or their eyes would be downcast from fear of offending a guest with their attention. Here they enjoy the chance to be a part of this, even if it means they carry trays of food and drink to serve others."

"Huh," she said, following one woman across the room with her eyes. The server smiled genuinely at each person she looked at and seemed happy when someone selected a glass from her tray. "I never noticed that before."

"You haven't had a lifetime of watching everyone to find your target. Picking up on people's emotions and reactions becomes second nature."

"Kole, do you like being a bounty hunter?"

He barked a laugh. "I like the thrill of finding people that others can't. Chasing them down to even the darkest corners of the galaxy. There's a joy in succeeding that's hard to match."

"Do you ever feel bad for those people you track down? They had to have a reason to run away, like. Can't all be criminals, yeah?"

He shrugged. "Some aren't, that's true. But they've all done something to make people want them found. It's not my job to ask *why* I'm hired. I only get paid to find the bounty."

"I just think you should consider it, man. Could be doing some bad things, like." Her voice had gotten very low. Sad.

Kole was about to ask if she had experience with bounty hunters taking someone that was close, but the group he'd been watching suddenly broke apart. Two of the women started to wander along the table heaped with food, while the others trickled from the room at varying rates. In a way that suggested they didn't want people to guess they were together.

It was suspicious enough that he felt compelled to follow some of them. "Keep an eye on those women," he said under his breath, surreptitiously pointing them out to Neela. "I'll find you."

She started to say something, but he couldn't lose time. The three he wanted to follow were already leaving the room, and his own adopted pace was too slow to keep up easily. He started hobbling as quickly as he felt was safe, leaving the dining room in time to see that the three had gone entirely different directions. One man disappeared into the crowd in the foyer, the woman had gone the opposite way down the hall toward a room with a closed door, and the second man had crossed into the ballroom.

Since it was closest and the easiest location to reach, Kole followed the last man. The ballroom was laid out with a row of tables to either side. A small, elevated platform was set up in a far corner, where an eight-person band was playing softly gentle music. Perhaps a dozen couples filled the open space, dancing closely.

Kole hobbled to the nearest chair and fell into it as if he were exhausted, letting his eyes sweep the room. He finally found his target, and he watched as the man weaved through the dancers to reach the tables on the other side of the ballroom. Once there, the man bent over a table to speak with another woman seated all alone. She looked incredibly similar to the man, making him think they were siblings.

A server passed by, and Kole held up a hand to stop him. The server lowered the tray so he could easily grab a fresh glass of clear wine, then bent lower as Kole beckoned him in. "Would you happen to know who that young man is?" he asked in a wavering voice.

The server glanced around, finding the table Kole was pointing to. "That's Thom Pendleton, sir, the son of your host." He looked almost confused that Kole hadn't known that already. "And his sister, of course. Tara Pendleton."

"Ah, of course! That's why they look so familiar. So hard to keep track of my memories these days." The server gave him a pitying smile, then turned away to continue his circuit of the room.

So, the scion of the family was plotting something with the people he'd been huddling with in the dining room. That made it much more likely to be some sort of local politics or family dispute. Boring and unrelated to an assassin trying to kill him.

Two people brushed past his seat, and he was surprised to see the two women he'd left Neela to watch. The young woman entered soon after, searching the room until she found him and then hurrying over. "Why did you want me to watch them, Kole? All they do is eat and giggle like little girls."

He grunted, now convinced he'd let his paranoia attach his attention to something unimportant. Probably even something as uninteresting as arranging a sexual dalliance. "I thought they were acting a bit suspicious." He waved her to the seat beside him, then leaned on the table to nod in the direction of the Pendleton siblings. "The son and daughter of our host. They appear around your age, if you'd like to go over and try to chat with them."

She turned to him with hooded eyes. "Because I'll get bored being attached to the old man?"

"Somewhat," he said with a smile. "Also, because it will give me an excuse to make myself scarce. I think we've been here long enough."

Neela nodded, her lips pushed out in thought. "Not quite yet," she said, surprising him by jumping up and grabbing his hand. She pulled him toward the dance floor, ignoring his attempted protests. "You brought me to a party, and we're not leaving until I get to dance."

"I'm sure any number of young men would greatly enjoy a chance to dance with a beautiful young woman," he said, trying to sway along with her while maintaining his decrepit disguise.

"You think I'm beautiful?"

141

"I'd have to be blind to think otherwise," he said, looking around to judge reactions to his dancing. He was slow to realize her steps had faltered, and he looked down to see eyes brimming with tears.

"I didn't think you'd ever notice me," she said with a happy smile.

Before he could think of a response, she went up on her toes to brush her lips against his. Then she walked away, in the direction of the table where the Pendleton siblings were now holding court with other party guests around their age.

Kole was confused about what had just happened, but he couldn't afford to stand there looking more senile than at least one server already thought he was. He turned to hobble out of the ballroom, stopping a passing server to ask if there was a place he could rest in quiet. She was kind enough to take his arm and guide him along the hall.

He was taken into the room at the end of the hall that he'd seen one of the women disappear into earlier. It was a lounge with small groups seated on plush couches where they could talk in private. The server took him through the room to a small nook that could be curtained off. She helped him get settled into a large chair, and pulled the curtain closed as she left with his thanks.

It was the perfect place, as if the server had known his true intentions and led him there purposefully. The curtain blocked off the view of anyone else in the room, and let others know someone didn't wish to be disturbed. Best of all, the window his chair faced led right out onto the lawn closest to the fence that separated the Pendleton and Welkins estates.

CHAPTER EIGHTEEN

There were no sensors on the window, or they'd been disabled for the evening of the party. He could imagine guests often did things like open a window to get a breath of fresh air, and no one would expect wealthy charity donors to have ulterior motives. Whatever the case, he was glad for it as he slipped out of his tuxedo. Underneath, he was wearing a black skintight biosuit that he always wore on jobs. It monitored his vital signs, provided a constant low-spectrum link to *Rim Jumper*, and had several other features that came in handy during jobs.

He pulled on a black face mask, to cover his temporarily white hair and pale face. Both would stand out far too easily in the growing darkness outside. The planet was rotating away from the sun, and full darkness was not far away. According to his research, Hebat Prime's rotation took seventy-three hours. The slow spin meant a longer day/night cycle, and also more solar radiation absorbed by each of the thousands of solar spikes.

The grass under the window was wet, leaving a trace of his footprints as he jogged away from the mansion. He considered wiping them away in some fashion, but it would take too much time. The fence was at least a quarter kilometer away, and if he was gone for more than an hour the risk of someone discovering his empty chair and discarded clothes grew too high.

He was beginning to huff as he approached the fence, made with the same steel bars he'd seen along the front of the estates. He'd been prepared to have to scale the stone fence that also protected the mansion, but he hadn't seen it. Apparently, the families didn't feel the need to protect themselves from each other. Only from the rabble that could come from the city if the citizens ever realized the power of coordinated protest.

Kole checked the fence for an electrical field first, yanking up a handful of grass and chucking it through the steel bars. The blades fell gently to the other side, and even those that were stopped by the bars suffered no ill effects. Exactly as he'd hoped.

The next possible obstacle was weight sensors. Were he in charge of the estate's security team, he'd want to know instantly if someone tried to climb the fence. However, such sensors were expensive, required a lot of maintenance, and could easily be set off by the heavier animal species found on most planets. He imagined the sensors were definitely on the bars at the front of the estates but was hoping the security here was half-hearted at best.

With a running jump, he grabbed two wide bars and began to pull himself up. It was four meters at most, a distance he could easily climb. Straddling the top of the fence, he listened for any sounds of alarm in the distance. Hearing none, he swept his eyes over the Welkins estate to see if there were any pitfalls he should be aware of. It was quiet and dark, however, with only a handful of lights showing in the distant mansion.

He dropped to the ground and began running for the rear of the estate. Kole angled toward the building he was just beginning to make out in the darkness, sinking to a crouch as he got closer. Even if the estate security was light here, if this was the assassin's docking location then they would have their own protective measures. Those would be nothing short of overkill.

Nothing happened as he drew closer and closer to the building. Stopping ten meters away, he deployed his best countermeasure. There was a small powerpack built into the spine of the suit, with enough juice to fuel a special electromagnetic pulse field for half a minute. He activated that and ran quickly forward. Any security systems within a short range would be disabled as they were overwhelmed by the pulse, and it was strong enough to get past all but the heaviest shielding.

When the pulse field died out, Kole was leaning beside the small entry set into the larger hanger doors. It was still quiet, with no signs that he'd been detected or that people were inside the building waiting to ambush him. He paused for a few seconds, catching his breath.

He pushed the door open quickly, rolling inside to come up where he'd be least expected. And then felt like an idiot when he looked around at a nearly empty building. The only thing filling the space was a personal yacht, slightly larger than a planetary cargo shuttle and built for maximum comfort. The yacht had a highly advanced and absurdly expensive FTL drive, but no weapons that he could see. It was also larger than the ship that had attacked *Rim Jumper*.

Kole cursed, realizing he'd just wasted a day going down the wrong path. Not to mention the twenty thousand credits spent to get into the party so he could find out he was wasting his time. He did a thorough search of the hanger, just to be sure that it wasn't being used to store another ship when the yacht wasn't in residence. From everything he could see, though, the Welkins hadn't used the ship in several years. Just another impulse purchase of the idle rich.

Exiting the hangar, he dreaded the return back to the house. Neela was going to ask him what he'd found, and he knew she'd be disappointed when he nothing to report. At least he didn't have to worry about security countermeasures this time. He took off for the fence right away, instead of heading back to the place he'd originally gone over. No point in the long route when he felt confident he could cross anywhere.

The yacht hanger was so close to the edge of the estate that he was over the fence and back on Pendleton property within ten minutes. There was still the long run back to the mansion, but as he was turning in that direction something caught his eye. There was another spacecraft hangar here, one he hadn't seen during his glider flights.

Kole approached the building quickly, knowing he didn't have time to adopt a cautious attitude. This building was smaller than its counterpart on the Welkins estate, perhaps half as tall and three quarters as wide. It was the low profile that made it harder to see from a distance.

147

He was rounding the corner of the building when he halted. A voice had spoken not far away, and then he heard an answer from a deeper voice. It was hard to tell, but both seemed to be coming from inside the hangar. Kole looked for a window he might be able to peer through, but as expected there were none to be found.

Moving as silently and quickly as possible, he got to the next corner of the building and bent to peer around it. The hangar doors were open slightly, enough for a bar of light to illuminate the ground in front of the building. It was a tempting sight, and he badly wanted to rush over and peer inside. He was about to do so when the door was shoved open a bit more and two men appeared. They stopped just outside, drinks in their hand.

"I think we finally got that engine cycle mismatch fixed," the first man said, turning his head up to look at the occasional shimmering flash from the energy barrier that was closer here than anywhere else in Prime.

"Yeah, but I'm not convinced that was causing the problems with the jump drive. Something in the FTL is bogging down in the middle of a jump, breaking the ship out before it should."

"Sure, but we'd have to take a test run to really get an idea. I don't see that happening."

"Not if we want to live," the second man said with a strained laugh.

Kole watched them enjoy the night air as they finished their drinks. When they retreated into the hanger, they pulled the doors tightly shut behind them. He cursed, unable to get a glimpse at what was inside now.

A glance at the small display on the forearm of his suit showed he didn't have any more time to waste. He'd already been gone longer than planned. Turning away from the hangar, he ran as quickly as he could back to the mansion. Finding the window he had exited from was simple; it was the only one open along that side of the house.

He jumped up, getting a good grip on the sill of the window and pulling himself through the crack that was only just large enough for his body. He wriggled to get through it, falling to the floor with a quiet thud. Breathing heavily from the run, he forced slow, even breaths as he twisted around and pulled the window closed. The latches on either side engaged without a sound.

The mask was the first thing he removed, stuffing it back into a small pocket on the inner thigh of his skinsuit. The fancy tuxedo he'd worn to the party was still bundled up just beside the window, and Kole grabbed the trousers. He pushed his legs into them one after another, quickly pulling them up and buttoning them at the waist. Then he shook out the white shirt, sliding his right arm into a sleeve as he turned to make sure the curtain was still tightly closed. It was.

He also wasn't alone. Kole froze as he saw the stony-faced young man sitting in the chair, watching him dress.

"I was wondering when you would rejoin us, Mr. Anwynn."

CHAPTER NINETEEN

"Mr. Pendleton." Of course it was him. Kole's first thought was that Neela must have said something that gave away his ruse, but he couldn't imagine her giving anyone his name. That meant the boy must have known who he was from the start.

"No need for formalities, Kole. You can call me Thom."

"I suppose it's your ship they're working on in that hanger?"

Pendleton laughed, a low chuckle that died quickly away. "Not my ship. However, the person it belongs to does work for me."

"And your sister," Kole said, shoving his arm through the other sleeve of the shirt.

"Yes, and Tara." Pendleton's smile grew a bit nastier.

"Then I guess you're the one I really want to speak to." Kole buttoned the cuffs of the shirt, sitting casually on the wide window sash. "Why did you send your assassin to kill me?"

"You should take it as the highest form of flattery, Kole. Your activities recently have been infringing upon our own business. People who pay us for protection have been complaining when you manage to find them and scoop them up. It can't be allowed to continue."

"That's it? I'm too good at my job, so you send someone to take me out?" Kole snorted, shaking his head as he picked up the black jacket and slung it over his shoulders so he could push his arms into the sleeves. "I suppose for someone like you, putting in effort to get better at your profession is too much to ask."

Pendleton's mouth tightened. "Tara and I are the best at what we do. You have no idea how many criminals out there are walking around safe because of us, ready to act on our orders at a moment's notice."

"Considering I've never heard of either of you, that's absolutely correct." Kole tugged on the sleeves of the jacket so that they were flush with the cuffs of his white shirt. At the same time, his fingers released the catch on two small sheaths woven into the fabric.

"You've been around too long, Kole." Pendleton's grin began to reappear, growing wider. "People like you are relics, convinced the Rim will always be the old-fashioned frontier that it was when you were born. Things change, old man. It's time for a younger generation to show you how it's done."

"Is that right, Thom? I'm going to guess that your assassin is older than you, probably closer to my age. Is that how your generation works? Hiring us 'old men' to do the work for you so you don't have to get your hands dirty?"

Pendleton growled, and reached up to yank the curtain open. A pair of armed security guards stood there, weapons drawn and held casually in front of them. "Since you were stupid enough to come right to me, I'm going to get rid of you myself. How's that for getting my hands dirty?"

"A good start," Kole said. "Shame you won't have a chance to see if you actually have the guts."

The first blade flew through the air with a subtle flick of his wrist, embedding in the right shoulder of the largest guard. The other raised her pistol and was close to having him in her sights when the second knife penetrated her dominant wrist. She dropped the weapon with a sharp cry of pain.

Pendleton looked at them in shock, trying to figure out how he'd lost the advantage so quickly. By the time he turned back, Kole had already thrown the window open and rolled backward to fall to the grass. He took off at a sprint, reaching into the pockets of his trousers to pull two more small knives free of their sheaths. As he ran, he tried to figure out how to get Neela out of the mansion.

He considered entering through the front door again, trying to find and extract the young woman before Pendleton could alert his guards to search the grounds. But that order was no doubt already going out. Slipping back into the house would be a death sentence. He had to hope they would see her as nothing more than a local he'd hired to show him around, not worth the trouble of hurting. She didn't know anything that could endanger them, anyway.

Shouts went up from the front of the mansion, as the guards began to spread out and look for him. Kole turned toward the boundary fence he had climbed earlier. If he could get over that, he could get away through the Wilkens estate. Especially now that he knew they weren't involved. Their guards wouldn't be watching for him.

A point that was proven very wrong a few minutes later, as blindingly bright lights appeared from the neighboring estate. Hovercars driving along the fence line to look for him. The Pendleton guards must have called the security teams on either side to ask for help, most likely claiming he was a thief or assassin. The two guards with knife wounds would lend credence to any such claims.

He reached through his white shirt, activating his skinsuit's computer systems. "ShANN, I'm in a little bit of trouble here. Any chance you can find an exit for me?"

"I have been monitoring your progress, Captain Anwynn. I am afraid that the communication channels in your area are overwhelmed with people searching for you."

"I know that, ShANN. I need to get out of here!"

"The neighboring estates are on high alert, as well, informed that you tried to assassinate the son of Terrance Pendleton, owner of Pendleton Energy Concerns."

"Great. Are they searching by name or description?"

"Description," ShANN said, letting him have one moment of relief. If Pendleton didn't release his name, it meant they weren't going to bring in the planetary security forces. Which meant everyone would be looking for his current disguise. He pulled the moles from his cheek, wincing as the glue holding them ripped his skin as it peeled off. The hair would be harder to hide, but the wrinkles were removed the same way.

By the time that was done, he was brought to a halt at the stone wall. It was as tall as the steel boundary fence, but smooth as glass. There was no way to climb this wall, and when he jumped up, he thought he saw short spikes across the top. He was glad he hadn't given in to his first impulse to jump and grab the top as he was running toward it.

Kole crouched down against the wall, listening to the sounds of hovercars on the Wilkens estate flying past several hundred meters away. Other hovercars were approaching from the direction of the Pendleton mansion. They'd be searching along the wall soon, and he could already see beams of light shining from the two guard towers that flanked the gate.

Forward and both sides were blocked to him. That left back, the way he'd come. Before he could think about how stupid the idea was, Kole turned and sprinted along the route he'd just followed. Amazingly, the hovercars searching for him were putting all their effort into probing around the stone wall. They didn't expect anyone to want to go deeper into the estate. Because there was no way to escape back there.

He slowed as he passed the mansion, but only enough to get a look at the people milling around the front entry. Thom Pendleton was standing at the top of the stone steps, his sister at his side as they talked to a man who seemed to be in charge of the guards. Half a dozen men and women surrounded them, weapons drawn and ready in case the bounty hunter should suddenly appear.

Kole paused near the window he'd made his escape from. For a moment, he thought it had been left unguarded. He could slip through and find Neela for extraction. But then he saw movement, and he realized someone was sitting in the chair watching through the window. He dropped to crawl through

155

the grass until he was sure he was out of the window's line of sight, then jumped to his feet again and continued his sprint.

There was only one option left for his escape. The last one anyone would expect him to use. The last one he'd ever have expected to be attempting.

His heartbeat was pounding in his ears as he fell against the side of the hangar. Pausing for a few seconds, he took deep breaths until his lungs weren't on fire any longer. Then he started to slide along the building, listening for any noises from within. He knew there had been at least two mechanics working on the ship earlier, though there could have been a dozen more inside he didn't see.

By the time he made it to the corner of the building closest to the hangar doors, he'd heard nothing at all. It was possible the mechanics had been called in to help search the grounds for him, but he couldn't believe his luck would be that good.

Kole crept to the small entry cut into the hangar door, holding his breath as he reached out. The door opened smoothly with the lightest pull and didn't make a noise. Once it was open, he waited for a count of ten. When nothing had happened, he ducked into the pitch-black space.

The light switch beside the door was unresponsive to his touch. He fumbled with the sleeve of his jacket, finally extracting the small stalk light that was hidden within the stitching. It was meant to help with close up tasks, but the small cone of faint light helped him to stumble through the building without slamming into the tables filled with loose tools or the parts scattered around the floor.

Soon he found a set of work lights, which must have been in use by the mechanics since they were still warm to the touch. Flicking the switch flooded the hangar with light, and Kole had to blink until his eyes grew accustomed to the new brightness.

Once he could see, he snorted and shook his head. The small attack pod he'd spent so much time and money trying to find was sitting right in front of him. It was two meters tall, four meters long. Shaped like a lozenge, with a gun port on the bottom that was currently empty but looked capable of holding a large caliber magnetic rail gun.

He walked around the ship, impressed with how the builders had managed to fit a faster than light drive onto such a small ship. It had to take up more than half of the interior, and it must have felt like riding a sled strapped to a rocket. The nozzles for the sub-light thrusters circled the ship, give it the ability to pivot and provide full three-hundred-and-sixty-degree movement.

Kole found the small door that would allow entry to the ship, but it was protected by one of the most secure locks he'd ever seen. There was a fingerprint scanner along with a genetic sampler. When he held his own finger up to it, he felt the quick pin prick, but nothing happened. It was a system designed to keep out anyone but the owner.

He turned his attention away from the ship, focusing on his escape. There had never been a chance of taking the attack pod, even if he'd been able to get inside. Much like *Rim Jumper*, he knew the ship's owner would have wired in remote access controls. If he'd managed to leave the estate in the pod,

157

it would have returned him within minutes to face the full complement of security guards.

What he wanted to find were the controls to lower the energy shield at the rear of the estate. It was normally an opening that lasted no more than the few seconds needed for a ship to enter or depart, but he should be able to configure something smaller that would last longer. Long enough for him to rush through it, out onto the unprotected surface of the planet.

Since Prime's sun was now on the far side of the planet, the solar radiation would be dropping. It would still be incredibly deadly if one were exposed for too long, but he should have at least three quarters of an hour before the effects created long-term damage. His biggest worry would be the cold. Without the heat of the sun baking the area, temperatures would drop low enough to induce hypothermia if he were exposed for too long.

Kole finally found the panel that controlled the estate's portion of the energy shield, and he cursed when he saw the screen was dark. He ran his fingers around the edges, looking for a power button or some kind of activation trigger.

"Are you trying to get through the barrier, Kole?"

He whirled to face the hangar doors, which were being pulled open as a handful of men and women entered. Weapons were pointed at him, and the faces of those carrying them let him know there would be no hesitation in pulling the triggers.

Thom Pendleton was in the middle of the group, smiling smugly. "It was smart of you to backtrack. Took me a little longer than it should have to think of that."

Kole looked around, hoping to find something he could use for a weapon. There were still the two small throwing knives he'd stuffed back into the pocket sheathes, but they would do little good against this many opponents. Pendleton didn't give him time to resist, holding out a couple of fingers and waving them in his direction.

Four of the security guards rushed him before he could pull his blades. Tree trunk arms wrapped around him, keeping his own arms tight against his body as metal binders were strapped over his wrists. The magnets within them were activated, holding his hands together with unbreakable force.

Meanwhile, Pendleton had strolled over to reach under the lip of the console and power up the energy shield controls. He sneered at the bounty hunter as he typed in a password on the display. "You've worked so hard to get here, Kole. I think it's only fair that we let you have what you want. A way out of Prime."

The guards around him snickered as Pendleton tapped buttons and adjusted settings on the display. It took no more than a minute for him to complete whatever he was doing. "There we are. Let's get Mr. Anwynn to his exit."

Kole was hauled from the hanger, two large hands pulling him along by their grips on his upper arms. He stumbled, trying to match the pace of the two guards leading him, and at one point his feet dragged along the ground until he managed to get them under him again.

Pendleton led the group toward the shimmering energy barrier, now a deep purple color that was almost black without the sun shining on it from outside. It was less than a quarter of a kilometer to the edge of the estate, and the group came to a halt several meters from where the energy field began. The emitters were set into a low steel wall buried in the ground, hundreds of them filling the half meter wide track that continued in either direction for as far as the eye could see.

Not long after they arrived, a small section of the barrier faded away. Just large enough for a single man to squeeze through. "Here's your exit now," Pendleton said. "Oh! I almost forgot that we're in the night cycle. It's going to get cold out there. You might want this." He pulled Neela's yellow silk wrap from a pocket, and the guards sniggered again as it was thrown around Kole's shoulders.

He was pushed forward, two of the guards propelling him toward the opening in the barrier. He tried to fight against them, but it proved useless. Snarling, he tried to turn and speak to Pendleton. A meaty fist slammed into his mouth, creating ringing in his ears as he was thrown through the opening in the barrier.

"Thank you for visiting Prime," Pendleton called in a singsong imitation of the spaceport announcements. "We hope we never see you again."

CHAPTER TWENTY

Kole felt the cold hit in the first moments he was outside Prime's protective barrier. It was already getting close to freezing, even though the sun had only dropped below the horizon a short time earlier. If he didn't already know how dangerous the unprotected surface could be, that alone would alert him to the trouble he was in.

His foot hit a large stone, tripping him as he stumbled forward. He managed to twist as he fell to land on one shoulder, wincing in pain as another stone dug into his side. Getting back up was a struggle, with his hands still bound in front of his stomach by the magnetic restraints.

Knowing he had to hurry, he turned in the direction that would lead him to the spaceport the fastest. It was a journey of more than twenty kilometers, one he knew he could never make in the short time he would be able to survive on the surface.

"ShANN, I could really use a pickup about now."

"I'm sorry, Captain Anwynn. My departure request has been denied by spaceport control."

He cursed but wasn't very surprised. Pendleton would have contacts in every part of Prime's governing and administrative hierarchies. All he had to do was tell them to keep Kole's ship grounded and ignore any warnings that might come in about someone outside the barrier.

The restraints were his biggest concern at the moment. Hebat Prime had surprisingly few native animal species, but those that did live on the planet were fearsome. They tended to stay away from the city's shield, but you never knew when some brave animal might pick that moment to go exploring.

"ShANN, I expended my suit's power pack earlier. I could really use another electromagnetic pulse right now. Any chance we can find a way to recharge the power?"

"As far as I know, Captain Anwynn, there are no power ports on the planet's surface."

Kole stumbled to a stop, a laugh bubbling out. "ShANN, did you just make a joke?"

"No, captain, I merely pointed out a deficiency."

He shook his head, resuming his quick stumbling pace. "What about the barrier itself? Could I use that somehow to disrupt the magnetics in these restraints?"

"One moment." He waited as the AI ran scenarios for such a situation. Something that would have taken fifteen minutes or more for him to figure out took only a few seconds for her. "There is a seventy-nine-point-three percent chance such an idea could work. However, there is also a fifty-two-point-one percent chance you would damage your hands in the process."

He groaned. Not the kind of odds he'd wanted to hear. But he couldn't see any alternative, and he needed free movement of his hands if he were going to have even a miniscule chance of surviving this.

Kole approached the energy barrier. There was a faint hum that was felt more than heard, growing stronger the closer he got. He realized he'd been angling away from it as he jogged, his subconscious telling him to create distance from the danger.

Stopping a few meters away, he held his arms out in front of him. He twisted his wrists as much as possible to present the restraints and protect his hands. Then he took short steps, getting closer and closer to the shield that kept radiation away from Prime city while also regulating the environment within.

He felt buzzing before the restraints made contact, a sensation that made the hair on his arms stand up. There was no heat emanating from the barrier, just the growing hum and a feel of static electricity on the air. Kole fought the urge to close his eyes and turn away as he continued forward.

There was a snapping sound, and in the same instant he felt an electrical shock shoot through his body. His vision went dark.

When blurry images began to reappear, he realized he'd been unconscious for a while.

Kole groaned as the pain of a headache started to set in. He was on his back, but his arms were thrown to either side of his body. "Yay," he croaked in celebration of breaking the magnetic lock. When he felt like he could move, he lifted his head to see the energy barrier a good five meters away.

"ShANN," he said as he rolled over and pushed himself up onto hands and knees. There was no response from the AI. "ShANN, can you hear me?"

The electrical surge must have killed the communication circuits built into the skintight suit he wore. Now he was on the surface of a harsh planet without any kind of lifeline. But at least his wrists weren't locked together any longer.

Back on his feet, he examined his hands in the faint glow from the energy barrier. It was hard to tell when the light source made everything look purple, but he didn't think they had suffered too much damage. There was only a little pain, and that seemed to come from the scrapes he'd suffered when he landed on the rocky surface after being thrown to his back. Unfortunately, there was still the weight of the restraints, each metal cuff around his wrists at least five kilograms of extra drag on his limbs.

His muscles felt tense as he started moving again. Spasms would run through his body at random moments. Movement seemed to help, but it was hard to judge when he was starting to shiver from the growing cold even as the electrical stimulation died off.

Kole had no idea where he was in relation to what was on the other side of the energy barrier. Approaching the city from above had let him see a hazy image of the buildings within, but from the ground he couldn't see a thing through the barrier. It was like a vertical purple lake with a rainbow slick of oil across the surface. He wasn't sure if that was because of the darkness of the planet, or the thickness of the field so close to the emitters.

The long and short of it was that without contact to ShANN, he had no way of getting back inside Prime. This wasn't a situation where he could just knock on a random door and ask to come in. The only places the barrier was designed to create openings were at the spaceport and on the estates.

An eerie stuttering howl sounded in the distance, and Kole winced as it sent shivers down his spine. Whatever made that noise was clearly some kind of predator. On a planet where the prey animals were dangerous in their own right. He started jogging faster, trying to move as quickly as possible while conserving energy so he could keep going.

Too late, he remembered Neela's yellow wrap. It was no longer around his shoulders, and he turned back to look along the path he'd traveled. It must have fallen off when the energy barrier shocked him, and his brain had been so scrambled he didn't think to look around before he left the area. It was too far now, and he couldn't risk backtracking for something that held only sentimental value.

Thinking of the young woman sent his mind spiraling down into despair. What would the Pendleton siblings do with Neela now that they thought Kole was out of the way? She had no value to them, and while there was no reason to hurt her, there was also no reason to let her go and risk her talking about anything she might have seen or heard. To people like the Pendletons, she was probably just another street rat that provided nothing to their bottom line.

She wouldn't go down easily, though. That was his one consolation. Whatever they did to her, she would fight them tooth and nail. Maybe she'd draw attention, make it pointless to hurt her. Best case, they'd release her hoping to put hired killers on her trail later on if she became a problem. And it was all because he'd taken a ride in her taxi and developed a foolish attachment to her.

Kole growled in anger, unsure if he was more upset with himself for getting her into the situation or because he was helpless to get her out of it. As he continued running, hoping to see a bubble in the shield that would be the first sign of a spaceport docking pad, he imagined all the ways he wanted to kill Thom Pendleton and his sister.

Another barking howl drew him from vengeful thoughts. This one was closer than before. A second howl followed behind it, from a slightly different direction. Kole grimaced and increased his speed. Sounds like that could mean only one thing. The predators had his scent, and they were hunting him.

His breath was coming harder as he ran, but the howls continued. They were still getting closer, whatever beasts that followed him moving faster than he could run. Kole put his head down and poured everything into his sprint. There was nothing to run toward, but he was damn sure prepared to run *away* from anything that made such chilling sounds.

He was beginning to sweat, his body heat rising with the exertion. The shivering had stopped, but he knew that just made the cold more dangerous. The sweat on his body would soak into his clothing, which would then start to freeze in the air and bring his body temps down even more. It was a cycle that would lead to hypothermia and death.

But only if he survived whatever was chasing him. He could hear a whuffing sound behind him now, and Kole had to

166

fight against the temptation to turn back to see what might be creating it. That would only slow his own steps and could prove deadly when he was having to swerve around large boulders so often.

A scream sounded not far behind him, similar to a human sound and yet instantly recognizable as coming from an alien throat. Scrabbling steps came from his right, and he turned his head just in time to see a creature leap from a boulder several meters away. Kole raised his arms protectively and fell to the dirt as the beast smacked into him.

Sharp teeth bit through his layers of clothing, piercing skin. The jaws locked in and started to shake his arm back and forth. Beady eyes looked into his, set into a skull that was smaller than he'd expected. The animal was only half a meter in length, with scaly skin covered in downy feathers. The three limbs pressing against his stomach were tipped with talons, two thicker hind legs bracing against the ground to either side of his body.

Roaring with pain and rage, Kole raised his free arm and brought a fist down on the creature's back. The first impact did nothing, but at the second the creature seemed to grunt. A glint of purple light caught his eye as he raised his arm again, and he saw the metal restraint still around his wrist. He redirected his next blow, focusing the force on the metal ring so that it slammed into the scaly back.

The beast released its hold on his arm, an ear-splitting scream coming from its mouth only inches from his own face. Kole shoved the metal restraint on his injured arm into the creature's mouth, using the metal to force the jaws wide. He wrapped his other arm around the thing's neck, pulling down with one arm while pushing up with the other. There was a loud cracking sound and the beast let out another piercing scream that wavered into a protesting howl.

Kole released the animal, gratified to see it scramble away. The thing's lower jaw was hanging loose, the cartilage or tendons snapped so that it was useless. The creature gave him an almost indignant look before turning and sprinting into the darkness.

He didn't have much time to celebrate, as another of the small beasts zoomed right at him. The beast's jaws were open wide, rows of deadly sharp teeth exposed. He noticed the thing ran on its larger back legs, while the three forelegs were held out with talons extended. Kole rolled quickly to the side, and the beast was unable to correct its course quickly enough to follow. It ran past him, turning in a wide circle to come at his new location.

He spun to the side again as it approached, this time rolling until he was close to a rock small enough that he could lift it with one hand. As the creature turned again to run at him, he hefted the stone. Judging the right moment, he swung the rock through the air to slam into the side of the beast's head a second before the teeth were close enough to latch onto his body.

The creature was knocked onto its side, scrambling to get back onto its rear legs. He noted with interest that only one of the forearms was put to the ground to help it up, while the other two remained held out in a defensive position.

168

Kole wrapped both hands around the large rock, raising it over his head and swinging it down with all his strength. Before the beast could get its footing again, the stone impacted the top of the thing's skull. It let out a pathetic bleat, followed by a whistling attempt at the scream it had unleashed earlier. The legs and forelimbs were twitching, and Kole raised the stone to bring it down on the creature's head a second and third time until it was still.

He fell back to sit on the ground, tossing the gore-stained rock to the ground with disgust. The smell of the creature's blood and brains was revolting, the stench strong enough to make him want to vomit. But that could also have been the dizziness that was growing worse by the moment. He looked down at the sleeve where the first beast had bit him, and he watched blood ooze from the wounds.

Kole realized that the creatures must have poison glands of some kind, or perhaps bacteria that was reacting badly with his human immune system. His stomach roiled and he turned to the side to vomit out the food he'd eaten at the party. A party that seemed to have been days ago instead of only a few hours.

Once the heaving had stopped, he reached up to wipe his mouth. Two hands were moving in his vision, and he couldn't make either of them touch his face. "Oh, shit," he mumbled, feeling his head hit the ground an instant later. The sky seemed to spin above him, even though he could see nothing but a faint purple light from the energy barrier.

And then he saw other lights. Bright lights that grew larger as he tried to focus on them.

A hot wind seemed to flow over him.

He wondered if he was hallucinating now, but the thoughts were too slippery to stick in his brain. The lights started to fade as his vision became more fragmented, and then he was in darkness again.

CHAPTER TWENTY-ONE

"Welcome back."

The gentle voice came from beside him, and Kole struggled to open his eyes and turn his head. As soon as his eyes moved, the dizziness seemed ready to take hold again. He groaned and squeezed them shut, opening his mouth to croak out incoherent words. A straw was placed on his lips, and he sucked up water to moisten his dry mouth. "What happened?" he was finally able to ask.

"You managed to fight off two zerg lizards," the voice said, amusement behind the words. "I've never seen anyone survive an unarmed encounter with *one* of them, much less two."

"Where am I?" He opened his eyes again experimentally. The room seemed to spin slowly, but as long as he didn't move his eyes too quickly it was manageable.

"My private medical suite. Zerg lizards have all kinds of nasty bacteria in their mouths, and a lot of that entered your bloodstream when you were bitten. The doctor is pumping you full of antibiotics to counter the effects."

Kole was able to move his head enough to make out the woman sitting beside him. His body tensed up, and he tried to reach out to her. His hand barely moved before it was stopped by the restraints still wrapped around his wrists. The magnetic locks had been re-engaged, keeping his wrist locked to the bed rails at his side.

"Sorry," the woman said with genuine apology. "You were thrashing around a lot in your sleep. The doctor said hallucinations and nightmares were common symptoms of the blood poisoning."

"Well, I'm awake now. You can release me."

She stood up to lean over the bed and meet his gaze. "That's what you said the last time, too. We released the locks, and half an hour later you were throwing people around screaming about someone coming to kill you."

Kole yanked on the restraints again, trying to remember being awake before this. His last hazy memory was the bright lights after he killed the second lizard creature. He'd been sure they were hallucinations, but maybe someone really had come looking for him.

"Why?" he asked himself. Aloud, he asked "How did you know to look for me, or where to find me?"

Cady laughed as she returned to the chair. "I got a message from Neela. It was short, but she told me that you got into trouble, were outside the protective shield, and needed help."

He relaxed a bit at that. "What about Neela? Is she safe? Did she get out of there?"

"Out of where? I haven't heard from her since."

"You need to find her." He turned his head to look at Cady, wincing as everything began to spin faster. "She's on the Pendleton estate. They grabbed her while we were undercover at a party."

Cady pinched her nose and squeezed her eyes shut. "There's no way my people could ever get onto an estate. Why would they grab her? What did you do to the Pendletons?"

"They're the ones who control the assassin that tried to kill me." He told her about the flyby of the estates in the glider, seeing the hangar building on the Wilkens estate, and then getting the invite to the party on the Pendleton estate.

"All of the founding families have private hangars, Kole. Do you think rich people travel with the unwashed masses on passenger ships?"

"I was searching there because of the trajectories of the attack pod's arrivals and departures. That came from the guy you put me in touch with at spaceport administration." He told her about stumbling onto the hangar on the Pendleton estate, how Thom was waiting for him when he returned, and the desperate attempt to escape.

"You left her in that house?" Cady asked, a frown on her face.

"I had no way to get to her. Believe me, I would have torn through those guards if I could have. Without any real weapons, my only option was to escape and go back when I was better prepared."

"She must have gotten away from them somehow to call me," Cady mused. "If Thom Pendleton threw you outside the energy shield, then he wanted you dead. He wouldn't care if your body were never found."

A doctor and nurse entered the room then, spending ten minutes checking Kole from head to toe. At the end of it, they decided his recovery wasn't going to be temporary this time. Once the restraints were released, and the metal bindings removed from his wrists, he enjoyed being able to rub the skin that had been chafing against the inside of them.

"I need to get out of here," he said, looking around for his clothing. The only thing he had on was a loose gown that tied closed at the sides.

"Not yet," the doctor said, gently pushing him back onto the bed. "I need to monitor you for at least another twelve hours, to make sure the zerg lizard bacteria doesn't come roaring back. You do *not* want to be wandering around the city when that happens."

Cady nodded, assuring the doctor that she'd make sure Kole didn't leave.

Once the medical people were gone, she opened a drawer and pulled out his freshly laundered clothing. "Get these on," she said, tossing them onto his chest.

He didn't ask why she was so eager for him to leave, just glad to be doing so. As he pulled on his skinsuit and white shirt, he fingered the holes in the left sleeve of each. Bloodstains surrounded the small punctures. He felt incredibly lucky that he'd managed to get an arm up to prevent the creature from locking those sharp teeth into his chest or face.

They left the medical sensor and IV line connected until the last minute. Kole yanked them both off and pulled on his black jacket as he followed Cady on shaky legs. She stopped at the door, looking out to make sure the hallway was clear before quickly walking out and turning right. He stayed close behind her.

The rooms they passed were all as nice as the one he'd woken up in, private rooms with plaques beside each door engraved with a name. He started to understand what Cady had meant about it being her private suite. Hebat Prime was definitely the type of planet where the wealthier citizens could buy almost anything.

She stopped at each turn to look around the corner, even after they were far from the room. Kole snorted. "I'm fairly certain our doctor won't be around here to see us leaving against his advice."

"That's not what I'm worried about," Cady said. She waved him forward as they hurried down another hall. She turned aside to push through a door that led to a stairway. When Kole looked back, the number beside the door was 124, white numbers inside a red box. They started descending the stairs, and Kole had to grip the railing tightly as his head spun from the exertion.

"Why are we trying not to be seen leaving? I'm sure the hospital won't care as long as they know you'll pay the bill."

"I'm more concerned about the Pendleton agents that will be trying to track you down. If I'd known they were the reason you were outside the shield, I would have taken you someplace without any records."

"You gave them my name when you brought me in?"

"Of course not," she said. "But the antibiotics required to fight off zerg lizard bacteria are only used for that purpose. It'll be a giant flashing sign for anyone who thinks to look for it."

Kole grimaced. It was the kind of information he would use to track a bounty, so he'd expect any half decent security force to think of it. "Would the doctors alert the planetary security forces when it was used? Surely someone authorized to be outside the energy barrier would have been in protective gear."

"It'll get reported, but I don't know that anything would normally come of it. If some idiot wants to wander around out there, whatever happens is on their own head."

They were both starting to breathe hard from the quick descent. As they passed another door, Kole saw 113 in a blue box beside it. He idly wondered if the color signified the type of space that floor was assigned. Mostly he hoped they weren't going to take the stairs all the way to the bottom of the building.

A few more levels down, he had to stop. His head was starting to spin again. Cady stood beside him, leaning on the rail to look up and down the stairwell for any sign of pursuit.

"Why did you come after me?" he asked.

"I told you, Neela called me."

"Why wouldn't you assume the people who tossed me outside the shield were the same people who hired you to spy on me?"

She turned serious eyes on him. "I sell information, Mr. Anwynn. I don't kill people. If someone who has hired me in the past tried to kill you, it wouldn't make me want to help you

176

any less. Besides, if the Pendletons are trying to kill you, then I'm going to help you. If I'd known the assassin worked for them, I never would have supplied any information about you."

"Bad blood between you?"

Her mouth tightened, becoming a thin slash in her face. "You could say that. It's a long story, and not one we have time for right now. Are you rested enough?"

"I guess so," he said, following as they started to go down the flights of stairs again. They made it another seventeen levels down, to where the number 96 was inside the first purple box he'd seen. Cady didn't even slow as she pulled the stairwell door open and led him into a hallway that split the large building.

She turned left, and almost jogged as she led him past the rows of doors lining the hall. There was a number next to each door, counting down as they passed. Cady stopped in front of a seemingly random door, banging her palm against it.

There was no response for several seconds, and then the door opened a crack and a white eye peered through into the hallway. "What you want, man?"

"It's Cady, Paolo. Open up."

The door swung open quickly, and the man behind the door greeted them with a wide smile. "Been a while, like. I wondered if you remember me here."

"I remember all of my people," Cady said with a smile as she patted his cheek. Kole followed into the small apartment, almost overwhelmed by the spicy smell of food being prepared. His nose twitched as he held back a sneeze.

There were several other people in the apartment, a woman and two small children that stared up at the new arrivals shyly before running away to another room. The mother smiled apologetically before following them, calling for the children to clean up before dinner.

Kole wondered for the first time how long he'd been in the hospital bed recovering from his time outside the energy barrier. It probably should have been one of his first questions, but this wasn't the place to ask. Was this family preparing for dinner of the day after the party, or had it been a week?

Cady and the man who'd opened the door were speaking with their heads together. The man nodded and smiled throughout, and she patted his shoulder before turning away to step closer to Kole. "Paolo is going to let you stay here for a while. I need to find out if anyone is searching for you, and I'll see if my people can find out anything about Neela. There have been no reports of any incidents at the party last night, at least."

One day. He felt better knowing he hadn't been out for longer. "I'd rather get back to *Rim Jumper*. My AI can help me run scenarios and find a way back onto the estate."

"Wait until I make sure we're clear. I don't need the Pendletons' people grabbing you in the street, and I'm sure they'll be watching your ship by now. Give me two hours. Three, tops. Then we'll find a way to get you back onto your ship and start planning how to get Neela off the estate."

He looked around the cramped apartment and sighed. "Two hours. If you're not back, I'm leaving."

178

She smiled at him and waved to Paolo and his wife as she ducked through the door and out into the hallway. The man motioned to Kole. "Come. Eat. We have plenty of paella for all of us."

CHAPTER TWENTY-TWO

He ate sparingly, looking askance at the bowl that had been deemed "plenty" and not liking the thought that he was taking food from the mouths of the kids that still stared at him in fascination from across the table. After half a bowl of the delicious paella, he claimed to be full. His stomach was making noises that disputed his words, but the family pretended not to hear.

Paolo and his wife kept up a constant conversation during the meal, talking about the latest gossip from the other families living on the floor. The wife, Julianna, told Kole a story about sneaking onto a residential level higher in the building. With wide-eyed astonishment, she told him about apartments that were so large one could walk a dozen steps between doors in the hallway. Such an extravagance of space was incomprehensible to the family that had worked so hard to reach their own meager position.

By the end of the meal, the oldest child had seemingly formed an attachment to the bounty hunter. She couldn't have been older than five or six, but as he stood uncomfortably to the side while the table was cleared, she put her little hand into his. She pulled him silently into a small room barely larger than a closet. Two pallets were made up on the floor, beds for the children.

The girl dropped his hand and ran over to pick up a thick tablet beside what must have been her bed. She held it up to him, pleading in her eyes. Kole took it from her, tapping the screen to life to find a children's picture book displayed. He sighed, checked the time on the tablet screen, and then decided that reading bedtime stories was as good a way to pass the time as any.

He crouched down beside the bed, where the girl sat with a ratty stuffed animal held tightly in her arms. Holding the tablet so she could see the screen with him, he started to read the words that displayed on the screen to accompany the images that appeared. He felt a weight at his side a few pages into the book, and he looked down in surprise to see the youngest child leaning against him to follow the story.

Once he finished one book, the oldest girl reached out silently and pressed an icon to start another one. Kole looked up when he heard low laughter, and found Paolo standing in the doorway. "You can stop whenever you want, man. They'll keep you here for days, like."

Kole smiled in acknowledgment and looked down at the tablet to keep reading. As much as he hadn't wanted to do it in the beginning, reading the simple stories for the children was erasing some of the stress and tension that had been building up for days.

He read three stories before he had to get up and move around. His knees were complaining about holding the crouch. It was also getting close to the two hours he'd given Cady. The small boy followed him out of the room, while the older girl stayed behind to play with her only stuffed animal.

Julianna smiled up at him from the chair where she was curled up with a glass of wine. "Thank you," she mouthed. Paolo was in the kitchen, preparing food for the next day's meals. Kole leaned against an empty stretch of counter.

"How do you know Cady?"

"I work for her long time ago, man. When I was young, like. I carried stuff for her, place to place. Good job, yeah?"

"You don't work for her now?"

Paolo laughed, and waved the knife in his hand toward his wife. "I met Julianna when I got older. Fell in love, yeah? She told me that I had to choose, the job or her. Easy choice, man."

Kole nodded, finding it interesting that Cady still kept tabs on a man who no longer worked for her. She had to be, to know where he lived when she needed a place to hide someone like himself. And yet the man hadn't been surprised to find her at his door. "Does she drop in often?"

"Cady a good woman, like," Julianna said behind him. "She come here every few months, look in on the kids. Good woman."

Paolo was nodding his head. "No matter what others say, man, if you in good with Cady she take care of you. Forever, like."

That didn't fit the picture he'd formed of the woman after meeting her at the Ice Palace the first time. Or when he'd figured out she was the one paying Neela to spy on him. He'd thought her no better than someone like Pulsar, caring only for what gave her the most benefit. Maybe he'd jumped to a faulty conclusion.

Several minutes later, the sound of a palm on the door echoed clearly in the small apartment. Paolo wiped his hands on a fraying rag as he approached and then opened it a tiny crack to look outside. Without saying anything, he pulled it open to let Cady slide past him.

"Okay, Kole, I've got a car downstairs. Pendleton's people are searching the hospital up in the 120 levels, but they didn't leave anyone to watch the service entrance. We can sneak out that way."

He turned to hold out a hand to Paolo. "Thank you for the excellent meal. You have lovely children." The fifty-credit chip in his palm was left behind as he pulled his hand away. It was the least he could do to thank the family for putting themselves in danger to hide him.

Cady poked her head out the doorway, and then waved for him to follow. They walked quickly toward another door at the end of the hall, one that didn't have a number plaque beside it. When she pulled it open, the smell of rotting garbage made his nose crinkle. There was a disposal chute just inside the door, the sides of it encrusted with months-old filth. A few lazy residents hadn't even bothered with the chute, just dropping their bags right inside the door.

Kole stepped over them and turned to where Cady was pressing a button beside an older-style elevator door. He could hear a mechanical whine behind it, and they waited for more than a minute before a stuttering ding announced the arrival of the car.

It was empty when the doors opened, and badly in need of a cleansing. Cady stepped into it first, pressing a button on a large panel as Kole followed her. The doors slid shut with a squeal, and the car jerked as it began to descend.

"I don't know why they want you dead, but they're pouring a lot of resources into finding you." Cady squinted as she looked at him. "The security forces have started asking around about you, too. Thom Pendleton must have some of them on his payroll."

"Great. Does that mean the spaceport officials could be involved?"

"Anything's possible. The people I pay to provide information haven't reported anything yet, but that could just mean they were offered more than I give."

"How do I get back to *Rim Jumper*, then?"

"You don't," she said with a snort. "I'm taking you somewhere Pendleton's people can't get access to. The only safe place I know of in Prime at the moment."

The elevator beeped, and the doors slid open to reveal a dark underground space. A row of beat-up hovercars were parked nearby, and the smell of garbage was stronger here than it had been above. A propped-open door revealed the source of the stench as the place where the bags dropped into the chute ended up.

One of the hovercars flashed lights set into the front of the vehicle. Cady lifted a hand in acknowledgement, pulling Kole along as she hurried over. The passenger compartment was large enough for both of them, and it was separated from the driver by the same transparent divider he'd seen in Neela's taxi.

Cady rapped the divider with her knuckles a few times, and the hovercar pulled out of the parking space to accelerate toward a ramp in the distance that would lead up to street level. Kole could feel his palms itching as they got closer. It was a sign that he'd long realized meant his intuition was trying to tell him to stop doing what he was currently doing.

Before he could say anything, a large black vehicle appeared on the ramp. It quickly swerved to one side so that the vehicle behind it could turn to the other. They parked in a V shape, and doors opened to emit several men and women who raised weapons.

"What do I do?" the driver asked, his voice filled with panic and fear.

"Keep driving," Cady said, leaning forward. "Straight through them."

Kole braced himself as the car sped up. The people standing between them and the exit seemed to realize what was happening at the same time, raising their weapons and firing at the vehicle. Rounds pinged against the exterior, a few shattering the glass in the windshield but not making it through.

They were thrown forward as the hovercar hit the two larger vehicles, shoving them aside as it slowed but continued toward the exit ramp. The driver's face was covered in blood, and Kole saw he must have smashed his nose against the control panel in the collision.

Cady groaned beside him, a red mark on her forehead where she'd slammed against the divider. Kole had managed to keep himself from a similar injury, but his wrists and elbows were aching from taking the brunt of his weight in the collision.

They swerved into traffic, and Kole snorted as he remembered how Neela had so casually done the same thing every time he rode with her. It was a little less fun this time, as they passed another large hovercar that was identical to those they'd just smashed through. It sped away from the curb behind them.

"We have a tail," he said, wishing the vehicle had a window at the rear. The driver pressed a button on his small display and got a view of the traffic behind them. The black vehicle, usually operated as a freight hauler, was swerving between the smaller vehicles around it. Getting closer to their own hovercar with every second.

"Take a turn on Seventh," Cady told the driver. "Then left on Callegas. You know that little garage we keep there? Get in there before these people can make that turn."

The car made a tight turn a few seconds later, and Kole had to brace against the door beside him. He kept his eyes on the small display, watching for the large vehicle to follow. It was only a handful of seconds behind them, but it lumbered through the turn and allowed them to increase their lead.

Not long after, the hovercar turned again. Even tighter this time, throwing Kole and Cady into each other as it fishtailed a few times. Just as he was getting his balance back again, the driver engaged an emergency brake. The car spun to the side, and then lurched forward into a garage opening, with the door already closing before they were through.

The hovercar settled to the ground as the engine spun down into silence. Sitting in the quiet darkness of the building as the closed door cut off any light, they all waited. The sound of traffic passing outside penetrated into the building, but there was nothing to tell them if they'd managed to get into the building before their pursuers rounded the second corner and saw them.

CHAPTER TWENTY-THREE

After a couple of minutes, Kole felt a finger poke his ribs. With a start, he realized he was still leaning heavily on Cady, almost crushing her against the door. He murmured an apology as he slid over on the seat. She was then able to extract a datapad from a pocket inside her jacket, which she activated.

"I can access the building's camera feeds," she said in a near whisper, typing in long strings of numbers and letters as she accessed security systems. Soon the screen of the small computer showed a view of the street just outside. Cars were passing by, but no one appeared to be paying more attention to the garage than might be expected.

Cady swiped to pull up another camera feed, this one on the building across the street. She sucked in a breath as it revealed the large black vehicle parked under a streetlight a dozen meters down the street.

"Did they make us?" Kole asked.

"I don't think so," she said slowly, cycling through a couple of other views farther down the street. "No one is outside the vehicle, but the rear windows are too dark to see the passenger area."

"What do we do? Is there a way out of here that won't put us on that street?"

"There is." She leaned forward, putting her mouth against a small slit in the divider as she spoke quietly to the driver, who was wiping blood from his face with a rag. He nodded his head a few times, then carefully opened his door and got out of the vehicle as quietly as possible.

Cady did the same with her door, waving for Kole to follow. The glow from her datapad screen offered faint illumination as they moved through the room that smelled of welding and grease. They passed a door set into the wall, and then stopped beside a large workbench covered in tools. The driver grabbed one side of it while Cady grabbed the other. They had to put some effort into it, but the workbench moved aside noiselessly on the mechanism that kept a trapdoor covered.

"Leads down to the tunnels," Cady told him as she typed in a code on the lock. "A section that we've never used for the Ice Palace or my other establishments, to keep people from stumbling through it."

The hatch opened to reveal a ladder with metal rungs leading down into a dimly lit corridor. Cady motioned for the driver to go down first, then Kole. She followed after them, pausing long enough to enter a code on a small panel just under the trapdoor after closing the hatch. He felt a faint vibration of the workbench automatically moving back into place to hide the entry to the tunnels.

Cady slid down the ladder, leading them confidently through the corridors. She stayed silent, and Kole followed her lead in case there was a reason to make as little noise as possible. Their driver was at the rear, huffing slightly as he kept up with them.

She stopped after what he'd guess to be two kilometers of travel, pulling an old-fashioned key from a pocket to slide into the lock of a door. She turned until it clicked, and then pulled the door open. Inside was a musty storage closet, filled with crates of spare parts and a couple of dented toolboxes.

"Help me with this," she said to Kole. They each grabbed one side of a storage rack and pulled on it. It scraped across the floor with a grating sound, revealing that there was a false wall attached to the back of the storage rack, so it blended in with the real wall. Another door was hidden behind that.

She unlocked it with another key, and then held her finger over a scanner before turning the knob to open it. Even as it swung open, a long row of dim lights activated to reveal a low, narrow passage. The driver closed the door of the storage closet behind them, which clicked with an automatic lock.

"There's no way to pull that rack against the wall to hide the door?" Kole asked, not finding an automatic mechanism like there had been for the workbench in the garage.

"No, but if they make it this far, they have some serious inside information." Cady shrugged. "That or I'm much worse at covering my tracks than I thought. Let's get moving, just in case that does happen."

She led the way again, with the driver again following at the rear. The ceiling of this new tunnel was low enough that Kole felt he had to duck as they walked. The passage was so tight that his shoulders were brushing against the dirty walls constantly. It smelled musty, like the kind of passage that was rarely used.

"What are the Pendletons involved in?" he asked.

"Too much," Cady said over her shoulder, the words almost echoing against the close walls. "They started out with a little money laundering and loan sharking, but then found other avenues to be more profitable. Now they run several drug operations and a few blackmail rings."

"Why? Their family controls one of the largest energy corporations on Hebat Prime. They must be rolling in all the credits anyone could ever need."

"Who knows? Some people always want more. Or maybe the spoiled little darlings got bored and decided to play at being bad. Whatever it is, they've proven to be quite good at it."

"Is Thom the driving force, with his sister just along for the ride?"

"Your guess is as good as mine. I've had dealings with the Pendletons twice. Once it was Thom who showed up to strong arm me out of an area in the city that he claimed they controlled. The second time Tara came in with honeyed words and soft looks. I get the feeling they choose who shows up depending on the tactic they feel will work best."

Kole chewed on his lip as they continued walking along the increasingly dank passage. The siblings sounded more dangerous than he first thought. They had large resources behind them, as well, even before their criminal activities took off. The one thing he couldn't figure out is how he rubbed up against them along the way, and why it necessitated sending an assassin to remove him from the equation.

Drips of water had begun to fall from overhead, and soon rivulets of moisture rolled along the walls, as well. When he saw the first patch of grayish-green mold, he was almost convinced they were traveling through ancient sewers. Prime was far too recent for such things, however. It had been only a few centuries since the planet was first colonized.

The air grew more humid, and Kole could feel moisture being breathed into his lungs. It seemed as if they'd been walking for hours, and his back was starting to ache from his hunched position. He was on the verge of asking for a break when Cady stopped ahead. She was looking up, and he craned his head to follow her eyes. There were arched openings above that he hadn't seen while looking straight ahead. Steel grates covered the small opening at the top of each arch, and Prime's purple twilight filtered down.

"We're almost there," she said after a few moments, then started forward again. Kole tried to see what she was looking at, but finally turned his head back down to look where he was stepping. After another hundred meters, the passage widened where a door was set into the wall. It looked sturdy and thick, built for maximum security. He expected to see an electronic pad beside it, but instead there was a simple series of number wheels. Seven of them, which could be turned to select a number.

"Too damp down here for electronics," Cady explained as she shielded the combination lock with her body and spun the wheels. The sound of the clicking filled the tunnel, until a deeper *thunk* signaled the locks on the door releasing. She spun the combination wheels once more to hide the code before pushing the door open and entering a new room.

"We wait here," she said once they were all inside and the door was closed and re-locked behind them. "My contact is meeting us, but it may be a while before she can get away." She walked over to a table, pulling out a thin drawer to reveal a handful of nutrient bars. Cady tossed one to each of the men, selecting one for herself and peeling it open.

Kole didn't try to hide his own hunger, ripping open the packaging on the bar and biting off a huge chunk. As he chewed the almost tasteless stuff, he looked around the room. The bricks seemed ancient, but looking closely at them he could see titanium mesh underneath where the veneer had chipped away through the years. It may have been designed to look old, but the room was built to withstand almost anything. They could probably survive an orbital strike from a capital warship in there.

Minutes passed, turning into an hour and then two. The driver of their escape car was slumped in a corner, his chin on his chest rising and falling slowly as he slept. Cady had plopped down in a hard metal chair, and Kole pulled one over to sit near her. "Thank you," he said quietly. "I never said that, but you saved my life out there."

She grinned and shrugged. "Neela's a special kid, and she likes you for some reason. I couldn't do anything but help you when she asked."

"And now you're prepared to risk your own life to help me save hers?"

"I am." She pursed her lips and grunted softly. "In all honesty, I still feel a little guilty about having her feed me information on your movements. I feel even worse about it, knowing that information was going to the Pendletons."

"It could have been someone else. There's no way to know if the person who contacted you was really the Pendletons' assassin."

"There's no one else I can think of that would pay that much. Or want it so badly. You may be one of the best bounty hunters in the Rim, Kole, but you're still just a bounty hunter. It's not a profession that strikes fear in hearts around Prime."

"*One* of the best?" he asked with a smirk. She chuckled in response. "So, what's the story with you and the Pendletons? I get the feeling you've clashed with them in the past."

She sighed, looking over at the driver. His chest was rising and falling slowly. "I used to be engaged. Years ago, before the Ice Palace and everything else. He was a good guy, Kole, so much better than either of us. Better than I deserved.

"David worked for the planetary governor. He was just a low-level aide, but he had access to the highest floors of the government building. That drew attention from people who wanted to use him in their own schemes. Two of those people were Thom and Tara Pendleton.

"Tara approached him first. She was young and beautiful, the daughter of the third wealthiest family in Prime, and he was flattered by the attention. Could you resist if someone like that

194

seduced you, Kole? Found reasons to be in the same places as you for several weeks, bought you drinks, spent time listening to you talk about your stresses and frustrations?"

"Maybe," he said. Then sniffed and smiled. "But probably not."

"Exactly. But my David did." She smiled wistfully, staring at the wall across from them. "He was friendly, but he rebuffed every advance as gently as he could. David told her he was engaged, and that he loved his fiancé. I don't imagine a woman like Tara Pendleton is told no very often. She didn't take it well.

"The Pendletons had planned to blackmail him. Threaten to tell me about his infidelity if he didn't give them access to government information. His strength of character ruined their plans, but it didn't take them very long to find a replacement. Four of them, actually, that I've been able to discover. One of them was tasked with a special job.

"Five months later, David and I were getting closer to our wedding. His parents were so excited, and it made up for my own parents dying before I fell in love with such a perfect man. We were already a happy family, even before I became an official member. Then one evening, a security forces squad showed up. They arrested David on the spot, charged him with murder and espionage. He was convicted within days, sent to an off-world detention facility. They wouldn't even tell us which one."

She grimaced, and her mouth puckered as if she was tasting something sour. "It took me a few years to dig out the details. Tara Pendleton had taken genetic traces from David during her attempts to seduce him. She used them to build a vegetative clone, and had her people use that body to leave behind tons of evidence when they killed a government official that was trying to crack down on their criminal enterprises. And then they framed him for the years of stolen information, something the internal security was starting to notice and look into. In one fell swoop, Tara removed a man who rebuffed her, and the Pendletons protected their other assets in the governor's staff."

Kole reached out to put a comforting hand on her shoulder, surprised to see a grim look on her face instead of the tears he might have expected. He thought there was more to the story, events that unfolded after that arrest.

Before he could ask, the main door of the room opened with a low squeal and a woman in a white dress walked in.

CHAPTER TWENTY-FOUR

Cady walked over and gave the woman a hug. "Kole Anwynn, this is Mirin Blakely."

"Nice to meet you," Kole said as he stood to greet her. The dress looked expensive, as did her hair and face. That coupled with the distance they'd traveled from the garage which had been on the outskirts of the city center led him to one conclusion. "Of the Blakely family, I presume."

Mirin smiled, her thin lips turning up at the corners. "Indeed. You've heard of us?"

"Not at all, just a guess based on the information I have."

"I told you he was smart," Cady said with a nudge.

"Yes, I suppose you did." Mirin's eyes darted to take in the driver who was sleeping through her arrival. "Leave him. I'll have some of my people retrieve him later. He can find a place to hide out until this is all over. One way or another." She then turned on her heel, striding from the room.

Cady jerked her head, and Kole followed. Yet another tunnel, but this one was no more than a dozen yards in length before ending at a set of carved stone steps. He climbed them slowly, leaving the soft yellow artificial light behind as he emerged into the constant, purple-tinged twilight of the energy barrier. A swath of yellow-green grass stretched in every direction. The camouflaged door that closed off the stairs was set within the only low rise in sight. Even knowing where it was, it was hard to find the door within the unbroken grass once it was shut.

Mirin was already walking away, her steps measured but quick as Cady and Kole rushed to follow. Within minutes a house was in view, much smaller than the mansion on the Pendleton estate. He leaned close to Cady. "The Blakely family isn't as well off as the Pendletons?"

She chuckled and shook her head. "Not even in the same stratosphere. They're loaded compared to you and me, but paupers next to the other founding families. A Blakely ancestor was convinced the solar spikes wouldn't work as well as advertised, and only put up a few hundred while the other families installed tens of thousands and bought up all the available land."

"I bet the family loves him for that."

"Yeah, I'm going to suggest you don't mention dear old great-grandfather Oscar while we're here."

"Noted. How did you get involved with Mirin? Or is your connection with the entire family?"

"Story for another day," she told him with a smirk as they crunched onto a gravel driveway that circled a large fountain in front of the house. Sprays of water were shooting into the air, lit by an orange glow from lights under the water.

Mirin headed directly for the large double doors set into the front of the house. It was two levels, with an elaborate peaked roof. It almost looked like a small-scale replica of the

Pendleton mansion, and Kole wondered if all the estate homes were designed from the same template. He'd noticed on other worlds that the wealthier citizens had a habit of copying those richer than they.

The doors opened as soon as Mirin was a few steps away, with two women in white uniforms standing to either side as she entered. Kole followed with Cady, looking around the foyer with amazement. The space was stuffed full of antique furniture, displaying styles and fabrics that would have been popular in this part of the Rim when Hebat Prime was first settled. It would all be worth a small fortune now.

Mirin started up the broad stairs to the upper level, then stopped and turned to look at them. "Please, make yourselves comfortable. Cady, you know where the kitchens are if you're hungry." She then turned and continued up the stairs to disappear through a door.

Kole's stomach rumbled at the words, reminding him that he'd only had the bland nutrient bar after what felt like half a day of navigating the underground tunnels. Cady tugged his sleeve, and he followed her through the manor until they arrived at a large space at the back of the house. The room set up with ovens and food storage devices was as large as *Rim Jumper*'s cargo bay. It was hard to believe all this was used to feed only one family.

Several men and women were working on prep work for a meal, and they looked up with inquisitive glances at the new arrivals. Cady ignored them, crossing to grab a loaf of bread still steaming from the ovens. She set it on a small table to the side of the room, and then retrieved slices of meat and vegetables from a food storage device so they could make sandwiches.

Kole watched her slather a yellow condiment on slices of bread before putting meat and vegetables between them. Her datapad was sticking out of the pocket she kept it in, drawing his eye. "Can I borrow that?"

She looked down at it, and then wiped her fingers on her pants before handing it over. "Just don't do anything stupid. The Pendletons are going to have their people scouring the networks looking for any trace of you."

"I just want to contact my ship."

"What?!" She snatched the datapad out of his hands. "That's exactly the kind of thing I'm talking about, Kole. Do you think they won't be watching any comm traffic in and out of the spaceport? By now they probably have a dozen people watching your ship from every angle to make sure you don't show up there."

"You worry too much," he said, making a grab for the datapad. She successfully pulled it out of his reach. "The comm channel on *Rim Jumper* has the best encryption software available on the Rim. Better than most available in the Outer Core, as well. Even if they picked up on the fact that I was communicating with my ship, they couldn't tell where the signal was coming from."

Cady thought about that, completing the two large sandwiches and setting one in front of him. "Fine, I'll trust you on that. After all, if a bounty hunter can't cover his tracks then he wouldn't have lasted as long as you have. Keep it short."

He mumbled a thank you as he took the datapad from her. The first thing he did was set up a confidential system container before initiating his communication request. It would be wiped once he was done, preventing her from being able to pull his encryption keys. The ones that let the ship know he was the person establishing the connection.

"Captain Anwynn, I am glad to know you are still alive."

"Thanks, ShANN. Don't get too weepy on me."

"I am incapable of weeping, captain."

"Sarcasm is lost on you, as ever. Has anyone tried to breach *Rim Jumper* in my absence?" He pulled up the internal camera feeds through the connection, swiping through a succession of empty rooms.

"There have been no attempts, Captain Anwynn. However, there has been significant activity around the docking area."

He pressed a few buttons to change to the external cameras. At least four people were in view. One was holding a scanner toward his ship, their attention on a large display set up on a small table in front of them. He wasn't familiar with the equipment they were using, but he didn't like the look of it.

"ShANN, increase the electrostatic shielding. Whatever they're trying to scan, I don't want them getting any results."

"Of course, captain. May I inquire as to when you will be returning onboard?"

"Uh, not sure on that right now. I may have stirred up a hornet's nest, and now Neela is being held by the people who want me dead."

"You should endeavor to free Ms. Rokvar. I liked her."

Rokvar? Kole felt bad that he'd never even asked for her last name. "Yeah, ShANN, I like her, too. Could you investigate the Pendleton estate? See if you can find any records from the early days after colonization that could help us bypass their security. I'll reach out to you in a few hours."

"Very well, Captain Anwynn. I will search for that information."

He killed the connection, deleted the private system container, and then passed the computer back to Cady. She'd been able to hear the entire conversation since he didn't have an earpiece. "Good thinking on the colonization records. The estates were all built in the first decade after the energy shield went up. No telling what kind of secrets might have been forgotten over the last couple hundred years."

He nodded, chewing a large bite of the sandwich. He didn't know what kind of meat it was, but it tasted delicious. "Wouldn't surprise me to find some kind of escape tunnel or something under these places. Prime had to be a wilder place back then."

Cady flashed her teeth. "You bet it was. My grandfather used to tell me stories about when he was young, and all the crazy things that happened back then. Before Prime was a city of towers and tight living."

"What about that tunnel we followed to reach this estate? How did you know about that?"

"Mirin found it with her sister when they were kids. She showed it to me several years ago, when we started working together. One of those escape tunnels you mentioned, I'd bet."

"Surely we can find something like that to get us onto the Pendleton estate. We could go right under their security and come up close to the mansion. Then it's just a matter of getting into the house and finding Neela."

"And getting past the dozen or so guards guarding the entrances and walking the halls?" Cady asked with a raised eyebrow. "No, our only hope is to draw them out, somehow. Get them away from their precious estate."

"Hmm," he said, finishing the sandwich. "Maybe, but would they bring Neela out with them?"

"They would, if we offered them something they want more," Mirin said from behind him.

Kole twisted in his chair to look at her, standing just inside the kitchens. "And what would that be?"

A small laser pistol appeared from behind her back. "You."

CHAPTER TWENTY-FIVE

Kole looked at the pistol, calculating how quickly he could move if she pulled the trigger. Not fast enough. He was tensing to jump up in the hopes of disarming her before she could fire, but Mirin only shook her head and smiled. It was a real smile, not the tight humorless example she'd given when they first met.

"You're the person the Pendletons want most in Prime, Mr. Anwynn. We'll offer to exchange you for the girl."

Metal restraints slid onto his wrists where his hands sat on the table, and he turned to see Cady snapping them tight as she glanced at him apologetically. The magnetic field was activated in low power mode, so that his hands could move, but no more than half a meter apart.

Mirin sat in an empty chair between them, keeping the pistol loosely trained on him. She had been careful to sit far enough away that he'd have to give away any move to attempt disarming or attacking her. "I do apologize for this turn of events, Mr. Anwynn, but it is the only way to get Cady's friend back."

"Okay, let's say we were going to do that." Kole leaned back in the chair, trying to act unconcerned about the change in his situation. "Where would you offer to make the trade? I doubt you want them coming here. You definitely don't want to go to their estate."

"Absolutely not," Mirin said firmly.

"What if they double cross you, and don't release Neela?"

"They wouldn't dare. The Blakely family may not have the same clout as the Pendletons, but our word still carries a great deal of power. It wouldn't be worth the loss to their reputation."

"Yeah, those Blakely's are honorable people. Just don't ask them to help you save a friend, huh?" Kole gave her a hard glare.

Mirin examined him, then traded a look with Cady, who shrugged eloquently. Sighing, she rose from her chair. "Follow me."

Cady pulled Kole to his feet and pushed him ahead of her as they walked through wide corridors tiled with expensive stone squares cut and shipped from other worlds. Paintings and holographic art filled the walls, even some that he recognized and knew the astounding value of. If this was what the home of the poorest founding family was like, he wished he could have seen more of the Pendleton mansion.

Soon they entered a room set up with a long wooden table that had four chairs on either side. The chair at the head of the table was larger than the others, plusher and visibly more important. Kole ran his hand along the table, raw wood sanded smooth before it was shipped thousands of light years to end up on Hebat Prime. The cost of it would be more than he'd paid to purchase *Rim Jumper* all those years ago.

Mirin sat to the right of the largest chair, motioning for Cady and Kole to sit opposite her. She pushed the pistol over to Cady. "Keep it pointed at him until we finish."

"Look, you don't have to keep me in restraints. I want Neela back as badly as you do. Let's work together on a plan that doesn't involve handing me over to the people who want me dead."

The women shared a frustrated look, and then Mirin sighed as she pressed a series of buttons to initiate a connection with the Pendletons. They waited for several minutes, staring at a large video screen that showed a rotating logo of the family crest. It was almost a surprise when the logo was replaced by a sneering face.

"I see the bounty hunter survived. You might be tougher than I gave you credit for, Kole."

"You tried your best, Pendleton. You won't have that chance again."

Cady poked him with the laser pistol, hissing under her breath. He'd let his anger get away with him for a second on seeing that smug face. Mirin smoothly took over the conversation.

"Thom, you remember my associate, Cady McEwan. She and I share a fondness for the young woman that you and your sister are holding."

"Mirin, still clinging to your friendship with a reeker, are you? What would daddy dearest say about that?"

"It's none of your concern how my family feels about my friendships. We want the woman released."

206

"What would you be willing to give me to get her back? And please don't offer me something as gauche as credits. I have more of those than I know what to do with."

"We'll trade you the bounty hunter," Cady said, jumping in with urgency in her voice as she waved the pistol at Kole. "Give us Neela, and you can have him."

Pendleton laughed, throwing his head back with the extent of his amusement. "Oh, this is wonderful. You save the man from dying, only to turn around and stab him in the back." His laughter filled the room.

"We just want the young woman returned safely, Thom." Mirin leaned toward the screen, dropping her voice a few octaves. "Will you make the swap?"

"Sure, sure. Why not? She's no use to me, anyway. Screams and fights back when we try to have a little fun."

Mirin sighed and dropped her head. "Thank you, Thom. We can meet you outside the gates of your estate in…"

"No, I don't think so." Pendleton looked off screen, and Kole wondered if his sister were there, giving him direction. "Not in Prime. You'll meet us at Spike 19447. You know where that is, don't you?"

"Yes," Mirin said through gritted teeth.

"Good. I was concerned the Blakely family might have forgotten about it after all these years. Seventy minutes from now."

The video screen went dark as he ended the call. Mirin glared at the blank screen for several seconds, her lips twisting in her anger. "The nerve of that man. Forcing me to meet him in such a place. Stay with him. I'll send in some guards to take him to our transport." She strode from the room, slamming the door behind her.

"What's the deal with Spike 19447?" Kole asked.

Cady sighed, standing and walking around the table. She kept the laser pistol in her hand, but she lowered the barrel to point at the ground. "It's the last solar spike the Blakely family ever erected. Great-grandfather Oscar owned several thousand hectares around it, but he refused to spend more money on the spikes until the first hundred started to show a profit."

"Ah, so it's Pendleton's way of twisting the knife."

"Yeah, and it gets worse. Pendleton's grandfather was just stepping into a leadership role at their company around that time. He had his accountants put together documents that showed their own solar spikes were losing effectiveness over time. Then he arranged for those files to be 'leaked' to the Blakely family's company. Old Oscar couldn't sell his vacant land fast enough after that. The Pendletons picked it all up for half what it was truly worth."

"Ouch." Kole could understand how Mirin and Cady had become friends, with their shared hatred of the Pendleton family. What he couldn't figure out was why they would so readily turn on him and hand him over. Cady wanted Neela back as badly as he did, but Mirin wouldn't share that desire so strongly.

"So that's where the bad blood started between the families," Cady said. "More has happened since, but that's not my story to tell."

The door opened, and three armed guards entered. Two of them held their weapons loosely as the third, a large man with at least fifty kilos on Kole, grabbed his arm and pulled him up from the chair. Cady shot him a half-apologetic shrug as he was led from the room.

The group exited the manor through a small door at the rear, into a carefully manicured garden. Flagstones placed at even intervals formed a path through and around plots filled with flowering plants and shrubs from a dozen planets throughout the Rim. Kole thought he recognized a delicate white flower at the center of the main arrangement as an orchid found only on a planet at the very edge of inhabitable space nearest the galaxy's core.

Past the gardens was only bare lawn, sloping down to where the energy barrier emitters formed the rear edge of the estate. Just before that was a small hanger building. The guards guided Kole around to the front of it, where the large doors were already open. Inside were three vehicles, one small yacht for interstellar travel and two hovercraft that were wider and larger than the vehicles that traveled the roads of Prime. They looked like pleasure craft he would expect to take out on a lake if he were on a different world.

Mirin was waiting beside one of them, a handful of guards going in and out of it as they loaded some gear. She saw Kole and turned her back on him with a distasteful grimace. Cady was by his side as they walked toward the open ramp, and she wrapped a hand around his bicep as they walked up into the hovercraft.

"I know you're not happy about this," she said quietly enough for only him to hear. "Just cooperate on this, please. I can't leave Neela with those people any longer than necessary."

"Sure, hand me over instead. I'm just a guy you only met a few days ago. Easily forgotten."

"Kole, if there was another way, I'd go for it. But there isn't, and you know that."

He wanted to say that they could arm all the guards entering the craft behind them and launch an attack, but the Pendletons had more of them. In a fire fight, he'd put all his money on their people winning. And then Neela would have no use for them any longer.

Cady squeezed his arm before she let go, and he was led to a seat nearby. His restraints allowed him enough freedom to set his hands to either side of his legs as heavy straps were pulled across his body and locked in place. Once that was done, he could move very little within the seat.

Eight guards entered the hovercraft in total, followed by Mirin as she talked with the one who looked to be in charge before disappearing into a separate compartment. Two of them went with her, leaving Cady and the other six to watch over Kole. He was suitably impressed with how vigilant they were around him.

He ran his hands along the seams of his pants, grateful that he was still wearing the same clothes he'd gone to the party in. He felt the familiar bumps of a few small knives and smiled with relief. As long as Pendleton's guards weren't any better at checking for weapons, he'd have a way to fight back once he was in their hands.

CHAPTER TWENTY-SIX

The hovercraft jerked as it lifted from the ground and started to glide forward. Kole wished he could see into the pilot compartment, to watch how the energy shield was lowered to allow them access past it. Instead, the only things he could see were Cady across from him and the two security guards sitting to either side of her.

She had a grim look on her face, eyes on the floor as if feelings of guilt wouldn't let her meet his gaze. He kept his eyes locked on her face in case she looked up. Her body was rigid, and her tongue kept darting out to lick dry lips. She was still holding the laser pistol, her hands flexing on the grip. Nervousness or fear, he wondered.

Travel was smooth once they were moving. Kole didn't notice any deceleration as they passed through the energy barrier, and he didn't feel any shifting for hard turns in either direction. "How far to this Spike 19447?" he asked loudly.

Cady's head jerked up, her eyes meeting his and then darting away. "About thirty minutes," she said. She pulled her datapad out of her pocket to wake the screen. "The meeting is in just under forty minutes, so we'll probably go slow so as to not arrive early."

"Wouldn't it be better to get there early? Get the lay of the land before the Pendletons arrive?"

One of the guards was nodding his head as Kole spoke, but Cady shook hers. "No, the agreement was to meet them at the exact time. We can't risk the Pendletons thinking we broke the rules already."

"Don't be surprised if they're already waiting for us," he said, leaning his head back and closing his eyes. He tested the restraints, pulling his hands farther apart. He got only a few centimeters before the magnetic pull was too strong to resist. The energy being fed into the field increased exponentially the farther he got from the allowed distance.

Sighing, he ran his eyes over the parts of the hovercraft interior he could see. Boredom was setting in quickly, and he could see from the unfocused expression on one guard that they were feeling the same way.

He woke from a doze after someone shoved his shoulder, and he blinked his eyes open in groggy surprise. He hadn't realized he was that tired, but it wasn't surprising. His body was still fighting the aftereffects of the zerg lizard bacteria, and he'd also expended a lot of energy in their escape through the underground tunnels.

Two of the guards released his straps and pulled him up, dialing up the magnetic restraints so that his hands were locked together in front of him. They kept a tight grip on his arms as they guided him up a set of stairs to a second level of the hovercraft.

Half of this deck was open to the air, and Mirin was already standing just outside the covered area. Kole was propelled within a few meters of her, where he could watch as they traveled over red dirt and large boulders. The craft would adjust course regularly to go around those too large to go over.

A hovercraft twice as large was already waiting ahead, barely visible in the pre-dawn darkness. There was a faint redness around the horizon that drew his eyes. Kole gasped in awe as the sun appeared at almost the same moment that the hovercar came to a halt. Within seconds, the darkness was gone as the first light of a new day washed over them.

Cady appeared at his side, following his gaze. "Sunrise is something you don't usually get to see on Hebat Prime. It's going to start getting hot now. Another hour, and we won't be able to stand out here unprotected."

"If the radiation doesn't kill you, the heat certainly will," Kole murmured, remembering how he had the thought while reading about the planet before he arrived. "You know they're going to kill me out here, right? Pendleton won't risk me escaping him again, and out here there will be no evidence to point back to him."

"I guess you'll just have to show him how dangerous you can be." She turned to look at him with hard eyes, then winked as she tapped a finger against the side of his leg. Not far from one of his concealed knives.

There was movement on the other hovercraft, separated from their own by no more than a few meters. Thom Pendleton appeared, along with a woman who looked remarkably similar. The sister, Tara. They were flanked by a dozen armed guards, though the weapons were all holstered at the moment.

214

Neela was between two of the guards, struggling as they pulled her along. Kole sighed with relief to see her unharmed. She was wearing different clothes, but her arms and legs were exposed and showed no signs of anything more than a few bruises. She stopped struggling when she saw the other hovercraft.

"Kole! Cady! Help me!"

"Shut her up," Thom Pendleton said without looking back. "Mirin, I wondered if you were going to show. Does this bring back memories?" He smiled nastily, turning his head to look up at the towering solar spike nearby.

Kole followed his gaze, watching with interest as large canopies stretched out to catch the solar radiation now that sunrise had come. They were slow to extend and looked like impressively large wings spreading to lift the spike from the ground.

"Let's just make the trade," Mirin said, pulling his attention back to the ground.

"Now, now," Tara Pendleton said, a playful smile on her lips as she leaned on her brother's arm. "We shouldn't be too hasty. I'd like to know why you're so eager to get this girl back? She has no uses as far as I can tell. Just a filthy little reeker someone put a nice dress on."

Neela let out a string of curses, kicking out with her legs as she tried to reach Tara. Thom looked back at her as he laughed at her futile efforts. Kole bit down on his tongue to keep from shouting in anger, while also feeling pride at the girl for still showing such spirit.

215

"It doesn't matter why we want her," Mirin said through clenched teeth. "We have the bounty hunter that *you* want, and her return is our price for handing him over."

"Yes, the bounty hunter that was taken care of until your reeker friend rescued him." Thom stepped forward, raising his sunglasses to squint at Cady. "The one who imagines herself some kind of mastermind. I thought you'd have learned not to mess with us years ago."

Cady started to step forward, but Mirin put out a restraining hand. "We're not here for you to play your little mind games. Give us the girl, and we'll give you Anwynn."

Thom lowered his sunglasses and shook his head. "You Blakelys are no fun. All business, and not very good at that." He looked up at the solar spike again as he laughed. Raising an arm, he waved his fingers.

The two guards holding Neela pushed her forward as a small platform extended out from both hovercraft. The pilots had positioned each craft so that the platforms could connect, forming a bridge between the vessels.

"Wait," Tara said as the guards were about to send Neela across. "I want the bounty hunter first. He's worth far more than some gutter rat."

Mirin looked back at her guards and gave a faint nod. Kole was led forward, and Cady walked over to meet him in front of the platform. She turned her back on the Pendletons, looking up into her eyes. "I'm so sorry about this, Kole. I couldn't leave Neela with the Pendletons, though."

"I want her to be safe as much as you do." He looked away from her, running his gaze over the men and women waiting for him on the other side.

"Thank you," she said, touching his forearm briefly. "I'm sorry it had to come to this."

"Me, too."

Shaking off the guards, he raised his chin and marched across the bridge to the Pendleton hovercraft. He thought he saw surprise in their eyes at the ease with which he gave himself over.

Neela was waiting on the other side, and she tried to get to him. The guards holding her arms wouldn't let her, though. "Kole, you don't have to do this, man. They're going to kill you, yeah?"

"I'd rather it be me than you," he said with a smile. "I'm sorry I got you wrapped up in this, Neela. I should have tried harder to get you out of that house when it all went to shit."

"No, man, this all my fault." She was almost in tears, her face scrunched up as she fought to hold them back. "They asked me questions about you at the party, like. I talked too much, and they figured out who you were."

"It's *not* your fault," he said, leaning forward. "They knew who I was the moment we walked into that house. You didn't tell them anything they didn't already know."

One of the guards stepped over, grabbing Kole's arm and trying to pull him away. "Neela, I'm the one to blame, okay? I never should have taken you into that place the way I did. I put you in danger, and I'll never forgive myself for it."

Thom groaned theatrically. "This is all so very touching, but can we please get on with it? Some of us have lives to get back to." He waved at his guards, and several others hurried over to help pull Kole away from the bridge. It was his turn to struggle. He wanted to make sure Neela was safe before they took him into the hovercraft.

Cady was calling for Neela, motioning urgently for the young woman to get to the Blakely craft. She looked back at Kole, and he jerked his head to tell her to go. Finally, she started to cross the bridge.

He breathed a sigh of relief, letting his body relax as he was pulled inside and thrown down a set of stairs to the lower level. The guards chuckled to each other as he rolled down the steps and landed on his shoulder with a grunt of pain. They descended slowly, pulling him to his feet by yanking the arm that he'd landed on.

"Go easy," he said, but they ignored him as they tossed him into a chair. He didn't have to wait long before Thom and Tara Pendleton appeared and walked down the stairs. They both had wide smiles as they looked at him, helpless before them.

"Déjà vu," Thom said with a snicker. "I don't think it's going to end the same way for you this time, however."

"Not at all," Tara said. "This time we'll make sure he's dead."

CHAPTER TWENTY-
SEVEN

Thom sat on one side of him, Tara on the other. They'd pulled chairs close to his own, forming a semi-circle looking through a large section of wall that had turned transparent with a wave of a Pendleton hand.

The Blakely hovercraft was already on the move, returning to the safety of the energy barrier before the radiation from the supersized star of the heart of the system could begin to take effect. Kole couldn't blame them for their haste. He wished he were aboard. With Neela.

"Amazing, isn't it?" Thom asked, waving expansively at the window. "You fight so hard to survive. You even become the first person to live to tell about fighting off two zerg lizards. And yet, your saviors drop you right back into my hands."

"It would seem the galaxy doesn't like you very much," Tara said, a smirk on her face as her eyes ran over his body.

"Oh. I don't know. The two of you are pleasant enough company. Almost as good as a couple of zerg lizards chewing on my arm."

Thom's smile slipped a little, not amused by Kole's quip. Or perhaps less than pleased with the fact that Kole was making jokes at all. Tara's smile, on the other hand, grew wider.

"Why don't you tell me why it suddenly became so imperative to kill me?" Kole asked. He relaxed in the chair, lifting his bound hands before dropping them into a more comfortable position in his lap. "I've never even heard the Pendleton name before I came to Prime."

"We wouldn't be as good as we are if you had." Thom said, false cheer returning.

"Very few people know what we're involved in," Tara added. "We work through intermediaries who have their own intermediaries. Layer upon layer, so the people on the street have no idea who they work for."

"Smart. I'm still not hearing a reason that I have to die."

"It's as I told you at the party. Your actions were impinging on our business. But the why doesn't really matter," Thom said, slapping a hand down on the arm of his chair. "This isn't some villain's exposition allowing our hero to escape his bonds."

"Algie will be so disappointed that you came right to us," Tara said. "He so hates when someone manages to survive a carefully planned attack. I rather think he takes it personally. He was cooking up all sorts of nasty little plans."

Kole scrunched up his nose at the name, a strange one that he'd never heard before. "So glad I could save you a few credits. Maybe in return you could just let me go and call it even."

Thom laughed, jumping out of his chair. "Afraid that can't happen, Kole. You've cost us more over the last year than we could possibly express. Plans that had been years in the making, expansions that would have eventually made us a power throughout the Rim."

"We'll still get there," Tara said soothingly, moving to stand behind her brother and putting her hands on his shoulders. "We just have to have a little more patience."

"I'll find that easier once our major irritant is removed." Thom held out a hand toward one of the guards standing against a wall, and the woman hurried forward with an electrical baton. "Hold him up."

Kole was grabbed by two large men, and they pulled him out of the chair. They dragged him into an open area away from the transparent window wall and kept tight grips on him.

Thom laughed as he stepped forward, playing with the switch that sent electricity arcing over the tip of the baton. He held it up in front of Kole's face, making him pull back and turn his face away. Thom laughed at that, and then pulled the baton away and quickly shoved it into Kole's stomach.

Kole grunted in pain, his body hunching inward in response to the electrical current shooting through his midsection. Pendleton held the baton against his stomach for several seconds before leisurely pulling it away. Kole gasped in air as his muscles continued to contract and release in response to the over stimulation.

"There you are, dear sister. He *can* feel pain."

"It sounds rather excruciating. Can I try?"

Tara came forward with quick hopping steps, taking the proffered baton as she danced around Kole. He watched her warily. Thom had attacked him with a gleeful look and smile, but Tara had a studied disinterest on her face that frightened him even more.

The first shock came from behind, when she was out of his view. He jerked backward in response, his spine straining against the muscle contractions. He clenched his jaw and held back the grunt this time, determined not to give them satisfaction.

Just as he was adapting to the pain, the baton slammed into his side. The electricity spiked through his organs, and he felt his abdominal muscles clench. It was almost enough to make him vomit all over the expensive rug he was standing on.

Tara danced around him a few more times, teasing him by shoving the baton forward but not making contact with his body. She giggled each time, though her eyes were still dead and emotionless. It suddenly came to him that she was putting on a show for her brother, trying to be like him.

Thom reached out to stop his sister, taking the baton from her hands. "I like seeing him suffer, but this is boring already. What else can we do to him?"

"Let's slice him open in a few places, and drop him over the side," Tara said, licking her lips as she turned to look through the window wall. "That will draw zerg lizards in a pack. Maybe even some of the jackals. I've never seen those in the wild before."

Thom smiled, holding out his hand until one of the guards placed a sharp knife in his palm. "I like the way you think, dear sister. And this time, we'll watch him until we know he's dead for sure."

She clapped her hands joyfully. "Can I make the first cut?"

He bowed, extending the knife as if offering her the chance to carve a roast at the dinner table. Tara took it, holding the blade up to turn it in the light. Kole was able to see the sharpness of the blade, the sheen on the metal that spoke of countless trips over a whetstone.

"I think we should start with a bit of blood," she said. She put a cold hand against his cheek, her fingers spread out to give a good grip. She held his head in place as she brought the blade up. Kole grunted as she sliced down his forehead, jumping over his left eye, through his nose, and then over his lips. A searing line of fire was left behind by the blade.

"My, my, my," Thom said as he held a finger to his chin. He examined Kole like he was looking at a painting in a gallery. "I do believe you've just ruined his looks, sister."

Blood flowed from the wound. His left eye was useless, the lashes already gummy with blood as he squeezed it shut. The taste of iron was on his tongue, making him squeeze his lips tightly to no avail.

Tara licked her lips again as she looked at her handiwork, and he saw the first flare of interest in her eyes. She was definitely the more dangerous of the siblings. Cool detachment coupled with sadistic joy in watching others suffer.

She held the knife up between them again, the blade now red with Kole's blood. Her gaze dropped to his chest, and he steeled himself to feel the knife slash through skin and muscle there. She lowered the blade deliberately, setting the tip

223

against the top of his pectoral. It sliced through his clothing with ease, drawing the first drops of blood underneath. Tara started to pull the knife down when Kole felt his face covered in lumps of wet something.

His good eye closed instinctively, and he heard shouted surprise and anger around him. The guards released his arms, and he almost fell to the ground. Kole raised his hands to wipe his face, looking down at hands that came away red with blood and pink globs of something else.

Tara was lying on the floor before him, one wide eye staring at him. Where the other should have been was a gaping crater, blood and brains oozing out over the shattered skull. Behind where she'd been standing was a small hole in the window wall, cracks spiderwebbing out around it. Beyond that, another hovercraft barely visible in the distance but growing as it sped toward them.

"Thirty seconds sooner would have been nice," he grumbled. He pulled his wrists apart, tired from having to hold them together since Cady had unlocked the restraints before he transferred to the Pendleton hovercraft.

He grabbed the knife from the floor where Tara had dropped it, and looked around to locate the guards. There were six of them in the room, all with their attention on the window where the shot had come from. Thom was being protected behind two of them. The man didn't even try to get around them to look at his sister, already accepting her death.

"It's the Blakely craft," one of the guards said, followed by a string of curses.

"What?" Now Thom was trying to look around the two hulking men he hid behind. "They wouldn't dare to come back and attack us."

Kole smiled widely, scraping along a wall as he moved through the shadows on the edges of the room. Pendleton was about to receive a lesson on how much the galaxy loved to disappoint those who felt themselves invulnerable.

"Tell everyone to start shooting at them!" Thom screamed, his voice shrill with panic. He finally glanced over at his sister's body, his hands trembling where they were supporting him against the back of a bodyguard.

Seconds later the cracking sounds of guns firing on the open deck overhead filled the room. Kole thought there must be at least a dozen people firing at the approaching hovercraft based on the noise, possibly more. The Blakely craft began an exaggerated weaving course, making it harder for anyone to hit any important targets on board. Several figures were popping up over the upper deck's railing to return fire.

Kole was almost in position now, having crept across the room without anyone glancing back to see what happened to their prisoner. They obviously thought his wounds bad enough to keep him out of the fight. He tightened his grip on the blood-soaked knife, reaching out with his other hand. A few steps more, and he'd be able to strike.

Pendleton turned his head at that moment, a stray movement capturing his attention. He kept turning his head, fear-stricken eyes growing larger as he saw the bounty hunter. He let out a shriek, slapping his hand repeatedly on the guard's shoulder.

Kole grimaced and jumped forward, trying to slide the knife across Pendleton's throat. Thom jerked back with panic-fueled adrenaline, only a thin cut across his tender flesh as the knife slid by. Before Kole could reverse his cut, the two guards Pendleton was hiding behind turned and pulled their guns around to point at him.

Hoping the noise of the approaching craft and continued firing from above would cover the sounds, Kole snarled and threw himself at the two guards. The shock of the sudden attack was enough to make them hesitate, and he was able to push both weapons aside before fingers convulsed on the triggers. The shots were close enough to conjure a ringing in his ears, but they went wide of their target.

Kole sprang up to wrap his legs around the torso of one guard, bringing his knife down in an overhead stab to bury the blade in in the soft spot between neck and shoulder. The guard yelled in pain and frustration, one arm dropping limply to his side as he kept trying to push the bounty hunter back with the other.

Two tree trunk arms wrapped around Kole's stomach as the other guard pulled him away from his comrade, a gun still held in one of those hands. As he released his legs from around the first guard, Kole ripped the knife away, leaving behind a fountain of blood. The first guard went pale, slapping both hands up over the wound even as Kole drove the knife down toward his own stomach.

The second guard let out yelp as the blade sliced across the back of his hand and down his forearm. The gun fell to the ground as it was released convulsively. As the arms loosened around him, Kole twisted and shoved the knife up through the other man's stomach. He pulled up as hard as he could, until the blade hit ribs and could go no further.

Something heavy crashed down on the back of his head. Blinding lights flashed in his eyes as he dropped to his knees, and he realized he'd left his weapon buried in the second guard. Kole looked up, intent on retrieving it, when the heavy something crashed into his lower back. He heard a loud snap, and hoped it hadn't come from within his body.

He was on his hands and knees when the kick came, a foot slamming into his ribs. Kole was tossed onto his side, sure this time that the snapping sound had been ribs cracking. Pendleton loomed over him, smiling now that he had the upper hand again.

"Not so tough, are you?" His foot kicked out again, colliding with Kole's stomach. "The big, bad bounty hunter."

The other guards in the room had been drawn by the commotion, and they surrounded Kole as he writhed on the floor groaning in pain, holding his stomach and ribs. Pendleton grinned, and kicked him again.

"Go upstairs," he told the guards. "I want everyone on the Blakely craft dead, do you hear me? We'll burn it to the ground."

Tom stopped them before they'd gone far. "No! We'll ram it into Spike 19447, destroy that with the last hopes of the

Blakely family." He was almost giggling as he came up with the idea, rubbing his hands together.

The four guards traded looks. Three of them hurried toward the stairs and up to the lower deck. The gunfire was just as furious as it had been in the beginning, the opposition from the other hovercraft more than they'd expected to face.

The last guard hesitated. "I don't want to leave you alone with him, sir. Let me shoot him. Then it's done."

"No, no," Thom said, holding up his hands and putting himself between the raised weapon and Kole. "I want to put him in the Blakely craft. Make it look like he shot them all and then died when it crashed into the solar spike. It's perfect. Two opponents destroyed at once, and his reputation will be ruined. We can start reversing some of the damage he's done to our business, dear sister!"

Kole and the guard both watched in confusion as Pendleton danced over to Tara's lifeless body. He knelt down, as if waiting for her to approve of his plan. The guard looked over at Kole, sighed heavily, and then turned and plodded up the stairs to the upper deck.

Pendleton turned back with a malicious grin on his face, and the beginning of insanity in his eyes. Rolling on the floor and letting out painful groans, Kole wondered if losing his sister had broken something inside the man.

"I really thought you'd be harder to beat," Pendleton mused, standing up and walking over. He stooped to pick up the weapon dropped by the second guard; the guard himself lay nearby in a pool of blood from his ripped open belly. "Tara always said reputations like yours were built on whispers and lies, but I thought surely there had to be some truth to it. I guess not."

Kole rolled onto his stomach, pulling himself away as Pendleton took a few steps closer. "You know, maybe I should shoot you somewhere painful, like the knee. The security forces will just think the people you killed over there" he waved the gun in the direction of the other hovercraft "got in a shot of their own."

Pendleton raised the gun, moving the barrel to one knee before swinging it to the next. "Which one should I pick? What do you think, dear sister?"

Kole didn't wait to find out what he thought the dead woman would tell him. He'd managed to reach his target, and he rolled over one last time. Before Pendleton even registered the weapon pointed at him, Kole squeezed the trigger. Twice.

Two red circles blossomed, one on Pendleton's chest and the other just below his ribs. The gun in his hand dropped slowly, as he looked down at himself with a look of wonderment. He swayed on his feet as the red circles began to expand and lines of red trickled down from them.

Kole pushed himself up, wincing as his cracked ribs sent a pulse of pain through his body. Along with his face, they were the only thing that hurt. Pendleton's kicks were surprisingly ineffectual, and it had taken every shred of acting skill he possessed to make it seem otherwise.

The dying man looked up, glazed eyes struggling to focus. "You... you're not... how..."

"Never underestimate your enemies," Kole said as he walked over and placed a steadying hand on Pendleton's shoulder. He guided the man into a nearby chair, settling him there before he could drop to the ground. His face was going pale, and his shirt was now soaked in blood from the wounds. The chest shot had missed the heart, but it must have nicked an artery.

"Tara... she said... you..."

"Tara's waiting for you, on the other side. No reason to stay here where life is suffering and pain. Just let go, Thom, and be with your sister again."

Pendleton tried to raise the gun that was still loosely held in his hand. The weapon flipped around as he did so, swinging on the finger that had been wrapped through the trigger guard. Kole put a hand on his wrist, pushing the arm down onto the couch again.

He kept his eyes on the stairs, in case the guards above had heard the sound of shots and came running down to check on their boss. It wasn't a surprise that no one appeared, with the fight between the hovercraft still raging.

Within seconds, the last of the light drained from Pendleton's eyes.

CHAPTER TWENTY-EIGHT

Kole grabbed both of the guns dropped by the guards he'd killed, before he ascended the stairs. No one was inside the covered portion of the upper deck, an area filled with shadows. He stopped and ran his eyes over the men and women crouching behind anything large enough to provide protection between shots.

Thirteen guards were visible to him, ten of them still alive and fighting. Three were splayed across the deck in varying poses, sightless eyes looking accusingly at their companions.

On the Blakely craft, far more than the eight guards he'd seen enter were firing back. He estimated at least twenty, though it was hard to tell with heads popping up for only a second before ducking behind cover again. He had to admit he was impressed with the subtle thinking of Mirin Blakely. Or perhaps it had been Cady's plan.

A plan he'd been unaware of until Cady released the lock on his restraints. From that point on, he'd operated under the assumption that there must be something more at work than a simple prisoner exchange.

He crept forward, crouching down until he was almost crawling across the deck. The nearest Pendleton guard was only a few meters away, behind all the others. None of them looked back, too absorbed in the dangers in front of them.

None of them looked back, as he grabbed the woman's head and twisted savagely until her neck snapped and she dropped bonelessly. One down.

Now he had three guns and his own protected position to fire from. Kole lined up a shot on a nearby guard, firing when the shots coming across from the other craft momentarily increased. Two down.

He twisted quickly, finding the next enemy and snapping off a shot. The man had been rising up to return fire, and the shot hit his lower spine. He fell forward onto the overturned chair he'd been using as cover. Three down.

His second shot was noticed, though, and a woman looked back at him. She let out a warning cry as he lined up his sights and put a laser blast through her open mouth. Four down.

Now the remaining guards were turning toward him. The danger at their back was much more urgent than the danger they had cover from. Within seconds, laser blasts were flying in his direction from the six survivors.

Kole ducked down behind the metal storage chest, which was bolted to the deck and thick enough to absorb all their fire. He knew he couldn't remain there long. Some of them had to have enough brain cells to realize they could circle his position and finish him off quickly.

He leaned forward, intending to sprint for the stairs down to the main deck. If he could draw some or all of the guards after him, it would give Mirin and her people a chance to get closer and cross over into the Pendleton hovercraft.

Two explosions went off behind him, the concussive wave pushing him forward onto his face. His ears were ringing loudly, and for a few seconds his eyes refused to focus. Kole shook his head to clear it, waiting for the shots to come as the guards rushed him.

When nothing happened, he rolled onto his back and looked around. Blakely guards were swarming across a make-shift bridge, a long metal sheet that was connecting the two hovercraft. The Pendleton guards were down, only a couple writhing and moaning as they recovered from the grenade attacks.

Kole forced himself up into a sitting position, pleased to find he still had a gun clenched in his hand. He opened and closed his mouth a few times, trying to clear the tinnitus left over from the explosion. As he did so, he watched the Blakely guards carefully. They surrounded the surviving enemies, two or three holding weapons on each of them until someone else could disarm and put the prisoners in restraints. None looked capable of putting up a fight.

Cady crossed the ramp, searching the deck until she found him. She hurried over with a tense look. "I knew I could count on you to cause a distraction, Kole. Getting them to back away from their cover a little opened them up to the grenades."

"Glad I could draw their fire for you," he grumbled.

She laughed, holding out a hand to pull him to his feet. "Are there more below? What about Thom and Tara?"

Kole shook his head. "They wanted to torture me. I disagreed with that idea. Now they're dead."

"Is that what happened here?" Cady asked, motioning at her own face.

He winced, having momentarily forgotten the cut across his face. The blood had stopped oozing out, and it was dried enough that he'd been able to use both of his eyes again. Kole reached up to gently touch his nose, wondering how badly it had been sliced. "Yeah. Tara was not a very nice woman. She took a little more pleasure in doing this than I expected."

Cady stepped closer, putting one hand on his shoulder while she raised the other to trace the cut. "You're going to need some stitches, but at least she didn't damage the eye. Ladies love a good scar." She winked at him as she stepped back.

A smaller woman barreled into him, her arms wrapping around him as her head butted against his injured chest. He sucked in breath, and she released him instantly. "Sorry, man, did I hurt you?"

"More like you reminded me of a problem," he said as he rubbed a hand over his ribs.

Neela looked up into his eyes, her mouth wide in an O as she followed the cut down his face. "Who did that? You need a doctor, like."

"We'll get him all the medical attention he needs," another voice said as Mirin joined them. She bowed her head to him. "Captain Anwynn, I apologize for our ruse of taking you prisoner. I knew it was the only way we could draw out the Pendletons."

"No need," he said, pulling Neela against his uninjured side in a hug. "I understand why you didn't want to tell me the plan. Even though I think I could have sold the whole prisoner thing quite well if I'd known."

"It turned out better than I thought possible," Cady said, looking around the open deck. Only three of the Pendleton guards were still alive, all with significant wounds from the grenades that exploded in their midst. "Kole took care of Thom and Tara."

"Well, I really only killed Thom. Whatever sniper you have on your ship took Tara down before she could do more than this." He waved at his bloody face.

Mirin smiled for the first time, the corners of her lips pulling up slowly. "Show me."

He led them down the stairs. Neela refused to let go. She seemed to think he needed someone beside him for support as they descended. He heard Cady chuckling quietly behind them and looked back quizzically. She only smirked at him.

At the bottom of the stairs, Neela gasped when she saw what was left of Tara's head, and again when she looked at the guard Kole had gutted. She buried her face against his chest after that.

Mirin and Cady looked at the four bodies with only flickers of emotion. Cady knelt over the two guards as Mirin walked over to the chair Thom was propped up in. She bent over to get close, and then whispered something at the body. Kole caught a few words, enough to form an idea of why the woman had hated the Pendleton siblings so much.

A dozen men and women clattered down the stairs, fanning out and leaving the main room to search the rest of the hovercraft. Within minutes, they returned at a slower pace. Weapons were holstered or out of sight.

The man in charge of the Blakely guards approached Mirin. "Ma'am, we're clear. Only three survivors, and they have been secured in your hovercraft."

"Thank you, William." She turned away from Thom's body. "What's the state of our own people?"

"We have three dead, ma'am. Four wounded, but only one is in urgent need of medical attention." He looked over at Kole. "Two, if we include this gentleman."

"He's not a gentleman," Mirin said with an amused look. "Very well, let's get back to our ship and return to the estate."

The lead guard motioned with a hand, and the others followed him to disappear up the stairs. Mirin was in the middle of the group, and she pulled Neela away from Kole to walk with her. They talked quietly as they went up the stairs.

Once they were gone, Kole started to hobble toward the stairs himself. He'd gone up a few steps when he felt Cady take his arm. "You know she's in love with you, right?"

"Mirin?" he asked in surprise. He thought back to the look she'd given him. It hadn't seemed all that flirtatious, but plenty of people in the galaxy weren't as overt in showing attention.

"No, you idiot." Cady slapped his chest, eliciting a groan even though she was nowhere near his cracked ribs. She looked up at him with a confused look that slowly turned into delight. "You really don't know. That's so unbelievably cute."

Before he could say anything else, she ran up the rest of the stairs. He looked around the room, shaking his head as he wondered if he'd ever figure out what the hell she was talking about.

His eyes stopped on Tara and the cavern of what was left of her head. He was going to have to find that sniper and congratulate them on such an excellent shot. A centimeter to the left, and they'd have missed. To the right, and he'd be lying next to her. That kind of precision was incredibly difficult from the distance that had separated the two hovercraft at the time.

Everyone else was already across the makeshift bridge by the time he made it to the upper deck. Kole took a last look at the bodies and damage around him, then followed to the Blakely ship.

CHAPTER TWENTY-NINE

Kole was able to appreciate the luxury of the hovercraft's main room this time, not being shackled with guards watching his every move in the hold. The Blakely ship wasn't as elegant as the Pendletons', but it was still incredibly comfortable.

In lieu of a window wall that could be transparent or opaque, there was a wall-spanning display screen. He watched the Pendleton hovercraft dwindling in the distance.

"What will you do about that?" he asked, waving a hand at the display. His other arm was being held by one of the guards as she examined his cracked ribs. His chest was already turning a lovely shade of yellowish black.

"Nothing," Mirin said from where she sat nearby, holding a glass filled with expensive liquor. "Let the security forces draw their own conclusions when they find it. If they ever do."

Cady barked a laugh. "Those two were so prone to disappearing for days at a time on unannounced trips, it will probably be a week before their family thinks to worry about them. Maybe longer."

"It'll be covered in zerg lizards or jackals by then," the guard examining Kole grumbled under her breath. She finally straightened up. "Just cracked, I think. Docs may want to get a scan of you when we're back at the estate, though."

He nodded in appreciation as the guard left the room. Neela took the opportunity to get up from the chair she'd been watching from, moving over to sit next to him on the small couch. She smiled at him when he looked over. "Thanks for rescuing me, like."

"I'd say the credit for that goes to Cady and Mirin." Kole leaned forward to pick up the drink that had been set on the table before him. "It was their idea to swap me for you. Otherwise, I'd have had to storm the Pendleton estate and risk them doing something stupid to you before I got you out of there."

"You let yourself be traded so I'd be safe, man. I know you better than you think, like. No way Cady could have taken you prisoner if you weren't cool with it, yeah?"

"I don't know, it was a bit of a surprise to see a laser pistol pointed at me when I thought I didn't have to worry about something like that. I suppose I could have fought harder, but I'm not sure it would have done much good."

Neela pushed air through her teeth in disgust. "No way, man. You a dangerous one, Kole. Everyone knows it. I've seen it, like. You'd have been out of there in no time if you wanted it, yeah?"

Cady was smirking at him from across the room. "Little bit of hero worship, like."

Kole snorted. He was definitely no hero. "It was my own fault you got caught in the first place, Neela. I should have expected that someone at that party would see through my stupid disguise. Better planning would have kept us both safe."

She laughed, turning to Mirin and Cady. "Should have seen it, like. Kole had these two big moles." She poked her cheek to show where they'd been. "Had a giant hair poking out of one, yeah? Grossest thing I've seen in a long time. Wrinkly skin, white hair. He looked like some old geezer in the reeks who can't afford the treatments."

He shrugged uncomfortably, reaching a hand up to his hair that was almost completely back to the normal color. The temporary dye had started to break down during the escape through the tunnels, and it was still flaking off like a very bad case of dandruff. "It wasn't all that great, apparently. Your own transformation was far more impressive, Neela. I almost didn't recognize you when I saw you on the hovercraft earlier. Even in those old clothes, you look so mature and sophisticated."

She blushed, looking away as she lifted a hand to run it through her black curls. A light clicked on in his head, and he jerked his head around to meet Cady's eyes. The woman was holding back laughter. She raised an eyebrow in his direction, nodding mutely.

Kole drained the glass of liquor, enjoying the burn in his throat as he tried to stop focusing on the new thoughts filling his head. He jumped to his feet, crossing the room to refill his glass and then leaning back against the small counter.

Mirin cleared her throat loudly. "Yes, well. Once we're back on my family's estate, our medical team will look at your face and ribs. I'm sure they can do something to minimize that scarring." Her looked turned mischievous. "You should still look presentable once that is done. Don't you think, Neela?"

"Scars are cool, like. Make you look even better, man. Dangerous, mysterious, sexy." She blushed even brighter, turning her face down to the glass she was holding but hadn't even sipped from.

"Yes," Cady said with a restrained laugh. "Scars are sexy."

"Well, I should check in with *Rim Jumper*," Kole said loudly. He was unaccustomed to feeling as awkward as he did at that moment, and he left the room as quickly as he could while maintaining his dignity. The laughter that followed in his wake didn't help.

Mirin had shown him her small communications room as they descended from the upper deck, and he closed the door as he entered it. He put in the codes to reach his ship and was happy to see ShANN's holographic face fill the screen.

"Captain Anwynn, I have been waiting to hear from you again. I have completed my search of the earliest plans for the founding family estates. There are a couple of options for entry points onto the Pendleton estate that may still exist. If you'd like, I can detail them for you now."

"No need, ShANN. Things took a bit of a different turn than I expected. We have Neela back, and the people who wanted me dead won't be chasing us any longer." He ran through a brief summary of everything that had happened since his last communication.

"That is excellent news, captain. However, I would remind you that we still do not know who the assassin is that tried to destroy both of us."

Kole was surprised his ship's AI would worry about that, but it made sense. Her own existence was tied to *Rim Jumper*.

Damaging the ship in deep space would have killed her just as much as it would him. It just might have taken a little longer for the reactors to die and the ship's systems to cease function.

"We don't, but I can't see them coming after us again without someone paying for the job. On that subject, I'd like you to comb through all the bounties I've collected in the last few years. In fact, go back five years. The Pendletons kept saying that I'd impacted their business with my work, and I want to know how."

"Very well, Captain Anwynn. I will have a report prepared by the time you return to the ship."

"That might take a while," he said. "I have to get checked out by the medical team."

"Yes, I would highly recommend that course of action. Your face does not look the way it should. Seeking medical attention is a good idea."

"Thanks, ShANN. Good to know you care." Maybe he should have paid a little extra for the empathy programming, after all.

"Will Ms. Rokvar be returning to *Rim Jumper* as well?"

"Why would she?"

"The clothing she changed out of remains in the spare cabin. I believe she expressed a desire to see more of the ship while she was here, as well, captain."

"Oh." He thought back to the hours before the party, but he could only remember her sullen silence. Something he hadn't understood at the time but could now. He cringed as he thought of how he'd taken her for a precocious teenager for so long. It was hard for him to do now, when she was no longer dressed in pink overalls with her wild pink dreadlocks bouncing with every step. Now he thought of her in that dress, with black curls surrounding her face like a cloud. It was an image he enjoyed far more than he liked to admit.

He cleared his throat, dismissing the memories. "Yes, I'll invite her aboard. Thanks for reminding me, ShANN."

He reached out to cut the connection, then remembered the camera views he'd looked at earlier in the day. "Are there still people on the docking pad, scanning the ship?"

"No, Captain Anwynn. They departed ninety-four minutes ago."

The Pendletons must have recalled their search teams once they had him aboard their hovercraft. No sense in so much effort when someone was offering to deliver himself without a fuss.

"Great. Monitor the spaceport for any other suspicious activity and alert me immediately." His hand slapped his empty thigh, remembering that his datapad had been taken away the night of the party. "Well, I guess let Cady know. Do you have her comm codes?"

"I do, Captain Anwynn, from when you contacted the ship from her device."

He left the room feeling lighter than when he'd entered. His ship was unguarded, the assassin was no doubt already looking for new employment, and Neela had been rescued unharmed. As far as he could tell, she had come out of the experience with only minor physical damage.

Cady was the only one in the main room when he returned, peering around the door before he entered. "Don't worry," she told him. "Mirin is giving Neela a tour of the control room. She said something about wanting to compare it to a cockpit on some old hunk of junk she'd visited recently." The smirk was back in full force.

He flopped down on the couch with a long sigh. "What the hell am I supposed to do about this? I spent the first few days thinking she was a teenager. I thought of her like a kid sister."

"And then you saw her as an adult, and you can't go back to your innocent thoughts?"

"Yeah, that. Very much that." He rubbed a hand over his face, wincing as he pulled at the cuts that he'd forgotten about again. "There's something about her, you know? She's so vibrant and full of life. Every time she enters the room it's like I see things in a totally new way."

"Oh, you've got it bad." Cady leaned forward gleefully. "Don't tell me the fearsome Kole Anwynn is at a loss about how to deal with a small twenty-two-year-old woman."

"I am completely at a loss," he admitted, staring up at the ceiling.

"I'm sure you'll figure it out," she said. Her tone turned serious. "If you ever hurt her, Kole, I want you to know that I'll be coming after you. I love that girl like my own little sister. You got me?"

"Whoa, let's not get ahead of ourselves." He held up both hands placatingly. "My work on Prime is complete. Once I'm patched up, *Rim Jumper* is heading out and I'm not looking back. I'm not the kind of guy who hangs around on a planet when a job is done."

She was smirking again, an eyebrow raised as she leaned back in the chair. "I know."

"Okay, then. Not much chance of me hurting Neela, is there?"

"You poor fool. You have no idea what's going to happen, do you?" She laughed as she pushed out of the chair, turning at the door to look back and laugh louder. "Men."

CHAPTER THIRTY

The Blakely medical team spent an hour working on his face. They stitched up his nose, attaching lab-grown skin grafts to cover the worst of the damage. The cuts over his eye and lips were lathered in regenerative salve, and then bandaged. He would still have scars, but they would be faint within a few weeks.

"The attack pod is gone," Mirin said as she breezed into the room once the medical team was done with him.

"When? Where did it go?"

"No idea on either. I wouldn't have known about it at all if I hadn't asked my head mechanic to manufacture a reason to check their hanger. He's friends with some of the people who work on the Pendleton estate, so they often visit each other. He couldn't get into the hangar, of course, but the doors were wide open and it was empty."

"The assassin must have known the Pendletons weren't coming back, and they took off to find greener pastures."

"That would be my guess, as well. They would have known where their employers went, and when to expect them back." Mirin sat on a stool nearby, leaning an elbow on a small table that had held the tray of instruments used to work on his face. "I don't understand why he or she wouldn't have been on the hovercraft, though."

"Assassins prefer to work from the dark," Kole said, lying back on the table again. His ribs gave a twinge, to remind him they were still cracked. The nurse had tightly wrapped his chest and told him not to get into any fights for a few days. Weeks, preferably. "They lose effectiveness if anyone discovers their identity. It's the main reason I was never attacked once I reached Prime. I was too close to home. Too high a chance for someone to observe it in such a densely packed city."

"Until you wandered onto their estate, and the Pendletons could try to solve their problem themselves."

"Yeah, what's the deal with that? Why do you rich people always get so tight-fisted at the wrong moments? I can think of a dozen ways a decent assassin could have lured me out of the city, but instead Thom tries to just toss me outside the energy barrier."

"The number one rule to having lots of credits is that you can't keep them if you spend it all." Mirin snorted a laugh. "Or so I'm told. I get a very modest allowance from my father, who still runs the company."

"I'm sure you'll get a bigger allowance soon," Kole said. With Thom and Tara out of the picture, the Pendleton family was suddenly left without a generation to take over the company from elderly parents. Mirin was already working on plans to propose a partnership with them, getting in the door before any of the other families realized the heirs might not be coming back. After a couple of centuries, the Blakely family was

poised to regain some of what they'd lost through great-grandfather Oscar's short-sightedness.

"Where is Neela?" he asked, trying to sound nonchalant.
He hadn't seen her since the trip on the hovercraft, when he'd
realized how she felt about him. At first, he'd been happy to
avoid the responsibility of figuring out how to handle that, but
now he was worried that she hadn't been by to check on him.

"She and Cady left as soon as we were back under the barrier. Something about big preparations."

"Oh." He was intrigued to feel a sense of longing and sadness at the thought that he might not see her again before he
left Hebat Prime. He pushed himself into a sitting position
with a low groan, and then looked around for his shirt. The
nurses had pulled it and the skinsuit off him as soon as he was
in the room, so they could look at his injuries.

"Restless, are we?" Mirin got up from the stool and
walked over to a small cabinet. She opened a door, pulling out
a fresh teal tunic. "Your own shirt was a total mess. I had it
disintegrated."

He caught the garment from the air and shook it out. A
little too big for his frame, but it would cover the bandages
around his chest. As he pulled it on, he wished he could have
had something to cover his face. "What about my skinsuit?"

"My people already sent it to the spaceport. It will be
waiting on your ship when you return." She crossed her arms
as she looked at him. "You should consider an upgrade, Kole.
That thing is at least five years old."

"It's served me well in that time. Without that suit, I'd have been lizard lunch when Pendleton tossed me out of the energy barrier."

"Hmm, I wouldn't be surprised if someone else convinces you to upgrade it."

"Not a chance," he sniffed. "If they ever release a version with features I can't live without, that's when I'll pay out for a new one."

She only smiled a secret smile, watching as he got to his feet and looked around the room as if trying to find a misplaced item. "I've arranged transportation for you. Don't bother telling me it was unnecessary. You have done more for me and my family in one day than anyone in the last few centuries."

"I'm the one who should be owing you. Without your help, I never would have gotten Neela back safely. Or taken out the people who wanted me dead."

"Interesting order to put that in," she said with a lopsided smile. "Call it even once my driver gets you back to the space-port. I assume you'll be taking off for some other world as soon as you can?"

He nodded as they left the medical room. Mirin led him through the hallways of the manor toward the foyer he was familiar with. "I burned through a lot of credits to save my own hide. Time to go pick up a few jobs to get back into the black."

They were at the double doors now, with the same two women in white uniforms holding them open. Mirin stepped over the threshold and turned to him. "Should your path ever lead you back to Prime, know that you have friends here. You can count on my family and Cady for anything you might need in future."

She held out a hand, which he took with gratitude. Then he walked gingerly down the stairs to where a hovercar was waiting. The driver was holding the door of the passenger compartment open, and Kole slid into the comfortable seat to relax with a sigh.

Kole pressed the button to turn off the heavy dark tint on the window beside him, so that he could watch as the car drove through the estate. The yellowish-green grass was waving in the wind of their passing. He tried to find the low hump where the door to the underground escape tunnel was located, but he couldn't see anything that looked familiar.

Past the gate, they entered the outskirts of the city. He kept expecting to see changes in Prime to reflect the changes within himself, but everything was just as he'd last seen it. Crowded sidewalks, glaring advertisements and shop signs, towering buildings that narrowed the world to no more than a few blocks at a time.

He was a little shocked to realize it was morning already by Galactic Standard time. Another day, the third since the party where things had gone so wrong. For a while, he ran scenarios in his head. Ways things could have turned out if he'd done this or that just a little differently. He never should have let Neela accompany him to the party, but he'd been unable to say no when she was so visibly excited for something. He'd thought for sure no one would recognize him.

The spaceport was bustling as they arrived. The driver pulled to the curb just outside the door that led directly to *Rim Jumper*'s docking pad. Kole thanked the man as he got out, and then pushed through the doors into the terminal building.

An announcement overhead alerted him that the passenger ship to Orion V was now boarding and would depart in twelve minutes. That explained the large number of people milling around. Orion was the center of the galactic government, home to the Senate and the Prince Regent who was nominally in charge of the million or so inhabited worlds contained within the Gar Hegemony.

Kole pushed through the crowd whenever it got too thick, ignoring the occasional complaint from his ribs when he bumped into someone too hard. One look at his face, and most people stepped back in shock or disgust. His left eye was covered with the bandages over his cuts, and he imagined he looked fierce with just the one eye glaring around.

A security forces officer hurried over to stop him near the exit to his docking pad. "I'm sorry, sir, this is a private ship. If you're looking for the Orion transport, you need to go down to…"

"This is my ship," Kole said. "*Rim Jumper*, I'm Captain Anwynn."

"Oh!" The woman had the grace to look embarrassed. "Let me get the door for you, captain."

"Would have been nice if the people trying to break into my ship could have been challenged," he grumbled as he brushed past her. He knew it wasn't her fault, but she was the only one there to vent his frustration on.

He stopped just outside the spaceport doors, drinking in the sight of the ship he loved more than anything else in the galaxy. Despite the multiple attempts to breach her, there was no sign of any damage. Running his hand along the cool metal, he made a full circuit of the ship. Ducking down to look underneath was harder than he liked with the multiple injuries, but he forced himself to do it every so often.

Once he was back at the rear of the ship, he pressed the keypad and punched in his security code. With a puff of air, the ramp lowered and he ducked his head as he walked into the cargo bay. That first inhalation of the smell of his ship brought a rush of nostalgia. Until that moment, he hadn't realized just how much he'd never expected to make it back.

"I'm home," he whispered, reaching out to pat the closest bulkhead.

He didn't hesitate as he headed up the sloping corridor toward the cockpit. He'd have ShANN check the job boards while they got clear of the planet, and they'd have a destination by the time they did an FTL jump.

A clattering noise brought him to a sudden halt. The noise had come from the second cabin. A noise that couldn't have been caused by items shifting since the ship wasn't moving yet. Kole looked back to the cargo bay, wondering if he should retrieve a gun before checking the cabin.

Another noise, this time a scraping sound like someone was moving a heavy container. He gritted his teeth, wondering how someone had managed to breach his defenses. ShANN should have warned him before he stepped onto the ship that there was an intruder aboard.

He took a few steps to the door of the cabin. If they were searching for something, he could take them by surprise. A weapon wouldn't be necessary. He settled his feet as he tapped the button to open the door, readying himself to jump as soon as he found the intruder.

The door slid noiselessly aside. For a second, Kole was disoriented as he looked within. Everything in the room had been shifted from where he was used to seeing it. Then he saw a small figure leaning over an open crate, digging inside of it.

With a snarl, he leapt forward. He growled as he wrapped his arms around the intruder and pulled them back from the crate. The person yelped in surprise as they both tumbled onto the bunk. Kole kept a tight grip, the intruder's arms locked under his. The person was fighting wildly, and then suddenly relaxed in his arms.

"If you wanted to get me in bed, like, you could have just asked."

The amused tone was the last thing he'd expected to hear. "Neela?"

"Yeah, Kole."

He jerked his arms away, releasing her. She didn't move from on top of him, and he realized her hair was tickling his face. It smelled wonderful, like flowery shampoo. He cleared his throat and turned his face away. "Want to get off me?"

"Not really," she said. But she rolled to the side, getting her feet under her and standing next to the bunk. She looked down at him with a mischievous look.

Kole scrambled to his feet. "What are you doing here? How did you get on my ship?"

She rolled her eyes, reminding him of the mannerisms that had made him think she was younger than she really was. "ShANN let me in, of course. How else was I going to get my things on board?"

"Huh?" He looked around and realized that the chest with its lid open was stuffed with clothing and possessions that he'd never seen before. The cargo containers that had been stored in the cabin were nowhere to be seen. Doors and drawers were open, half filled with neatly folded clothes already. "Neela, why are you putting your stuff on my ship?"

"Because I'm leaving Prime with you." She said it as if it were the most obvious thing in the galaxy. And for some reason, he felt that it was. He realized that a part of him had been almost expecting this. Hoping for it.

"Are you sure about this? My life isn't exactly the safest or most comfortable. What are your parents going to say?"

She was quiet for a while, her back turned to him as she shook wrinkles out of a pink skirt that she'd pulled from the chest. "My parents are dead."

"What? No, you showed me where they live, remember? 'Not up in the richies, but not down in the reekers.'"

She shook her head. "Just fantasy, man. My dad died when I was a little. His maintenance craft broke down three hundred kilometers from Prime. Couldn't get anyone on the comms. No one ever told me how he died, but I prefer to think it was the radiation.

"My mom wouldn't let it go. She was convinced he was still out there, wandering around, trying to get home. She went crazy, like. One day I woke up and she wasn't there anymore. Never came back."

He wasn't sure what to say to that. In lieu of words, he put a comforting hand on her back.

"I lived on the streets for a while, which is not a good place. Cady takes in strays now and then, and I got lucky when she chose me. She gave me a place to stay, even if it was a bunk in a room with five other kids. Without her, I don't know where I would have ended up, yeah?"

"I'm so sorry," he finally said. "How is traveling with me any better, though? I'm a bounty hunter, Neela. People try to kill me at least a couple times a year. I get paid to go into Rim World cesspits that you should never even be told about, much less visit."

"So?" She stiffened under his hand, straightening up and continuing her task of folding the shirt to put into a drawer. "You need me, Kole. Been alone too long, like, and forgot that everything can't be solved with hard words and violence."

He opened his mouth to deny that, then remembered how things had turned out on Hebat Prime. She had a point.

"ShANN agreed with me. So I'm going with you, yeah? Accept it."

He sighed, turning away to walk to the door of the cabin. "One trip. We'll see how things go, but don't get your hopes up. More than likely, I'll be dropping you back on this gods-forsaken dirtball in a few weeks."

Neela looked over her shoulder, her eyes shining with amusement. "We'll see."

* * * * *

I hope you've enjoyed Prime Example. Please leave a review if you have a moment.

If you'd like to get updates on what books are coming out, join my newsletter on my website. I also occasionally share short stories and previews of upcoming books for my subscribers.

Kole and Neela will be back soon with another Rim Jumper adventure.

OTHER BOOKS

Guild Series
Vagabond
Indomitable
Waterloo
Resolute

Jack Dahlish Series
Lost Souls
Memory and Sorrow
Dark Deception
Fateful Knights

Rim Jumper Series
Prime Example
Viridian Skies
Pirate's Nest

ABOUT THE AUTHOR

After more than 20 years of working IT support for a nationwide bank, Tim decided it was finally time to start putting his imagination on the page. Creating stories and new worlds has been second nature for him since he was a kid, and he has wanted to be a writer since high school.

If you'd like to keep up to date on Tim's projects, visit his website at www.timrangnow.com. You can sign up for his monthly newsletter there and get access to exclusive short stories and early peeks at upcoming books.